The Point of Light I

The Point of Light I

The Wandering Soul

Abboud Kadid

Published by Tablo

Copyright © Abboud Kadid 2020.
Published in 2020 by Tablo Publishing.

All rights reserved.

This book or any portion thereof may not be reproduced or used in any manner whatsoever without the express written permission of the author except for the use of brief quotations in a book review.

Publisher and wholesale enquiries: orders@tablo.io

20 21 22 23 LSC 10 9 8 7 6 5 4 3 2 1

TABLE OF CONTENTS

CHAPTER 1	1
THE UNIVERSITY OF KANSAS	29
THE SWITCH TO CONCORDIA UNIVERSITY	47
GRADUATION	77
ACTING	93
WORING IN DUBAI	105
MOVING TO TORONTO	109

CHAPTER 1

I used to live in darkness. I was searching for acceptance because I was angry at the world, but now I have eternal peace within, and I am not afraid of tomorrow. God has enlightened my heart. Because of the Holy Spirit residing in me, I have become a better family man. Salvation is a free gift and available for everyone. It isn't based on our deeds or acts; it is based on the blood of Jesus Christ on the cross. His precious blood paid for all mankind before and forever. **"For it is by grace you have been saved, through faith--and this is not from yourselves, it is the gift of God"**. (Ephesians 2:8).

INTRODUCTION

Sin is refusing to walk according to the Lord's will, and not accomplishing what he has already asked us to do. For example, it wasn't only Adam's actions that had showed disobedience, but also the thoughts of superiority and pride that had firstly occurred in their **minds** causing their lust to totally and gradually break through their **minds** and eventually followed by acting with the **flesh**. Unfortunately, by **believing** the fallen angel, the Lord was no longer their God.

(Proverbs 11:12; Proverbs 16:18; Genesis 3:1-7; Genesis 3:12-13)

My name is Abboud Kadid. I have been teaching English for 10 years, and I have travelled extensively. Moreover, I have lived in Europe, Middle East and North America. Also, I have met many different interesting people. On one hand, humbly speaking, God has given me the passion to be very **sensitive** to other's feelings since I was a young boy before being saved.

Later on, I have realized that the Lord had given me this particular personal trait to teach me about His Will in my life. On the other hand, not knowing and understanding His will in my life resulted in a wandering soul until I turned 38 years old, although the Lord had first **revealed** it while I was studying at the University of Kansas (Jay-Hawks).

Actually, I was 17 years old when I met one of the orientation's organizers. Later on, we ended up going for a church gathering where I listened to the pastor's message for almost an hour that same day. Actually, I was born a **Christian by name**. In spite of God's **repeated knocking** on our doors, we usually ignore his messages. **"Here I am! I stand at the door and knock. If anyone hears my voice and opens the door, I will come in and eat with that person, and they with me."** (Revelation 3:20). However, I started to completely walk away from God. Instead, I relied on my own understanding and experience reaching out to the **world's wisdom**.

Having done that, a feeling of continuous emotional pain and suffering had zipped through each mile stone of my twenty-one mile stones. Unfortunately, the level of **guilt and accusations** gradually and simultaneously increased until they had almost successfully started taking away most of the positive personal qualities I used to have; such as feelings of love, joy, peace, patience, restraint, kindness and gentleness. Other important attributes made up of respecting my parents and dealing honestly with my friends began fading away.

Nevertheless, God has always had a **plan** to save us." **For God so loved the world that he gave his one and only Son, that whoever believes in him shall not perish but have eternal life.** (John 3:16). So, the evil chain of being blamed inevitably resulted in **physically hurting myself** a couple of times until I met a well-respected Egyptian pediatrician at 4:00 am while living in Riyadh, Saudi Arabia.

I was thirty-eight-year-old family man with an **empty soul** that had been wandering asking to **hear God's words**. He talks to us through our **minds and our spirits** in whom the **Holy Spirit resides**. "One who was there had been an invalid for thirty-eight years. When Jesus saw him lying there and learned that he had been in this condition for a long time, he asked him, "Do you want to get well?" (John 5:5-6).

A. BABYHOOD (1-36 MONTHS)

"**Children are a heritage from the Lord, offspring a reward from him.**" (Psalm 127:3).

The moment God decides to give us life on this earth, our parents are responsible for getting us blended in as the newest member of their family. They have got only 2 options either applying their own **worldly life** experience or relying on **the Lord** through a combination of reading the Bible, praying and even fasting.

Frankly speaking, followers of the former choice believe that having an excellent job and a happy family with a good health are sufficient. Their **lives' purpose** defined by their own knowledge which directly affects their judgements, so God's real reason for their existence is left aside for a while until needed in case of **an emergency landing**.

Moreover, bringing up their newborn is may be explained through **life circumstances** exclusively. Some common statements uttered by parents mimicking the world, "Life isn't fair", "**He** wasn't there when we were penniless suffering for years", "**He** sometimes doesn't respond to our prayers", etc… Some even deny **His** existence. Most of those claims are human-made for **entertainment** purposes or they are just part of the never-ending repeated and meaningless discussions.

I have done some fairly objective research, and there is sufficient evidence proving otherwise:

Firstly, 7.8 billion is the current world population. Secondly, more than seven million species of plants and animals live on planet earth, according to estimates made by biologists with **Vertebrate & Invertebrate** animals and **plants**. Thirdly, recent estimates predict that there is between 100 to 200 billion galaxies in the universe, each of which has hundreds of billions of stars. In fact, a supercomputer suggests that the real number could reach **500 billion**.

Fourthly, a preliminary incomplete estimate of human total cell number calculated for a variety of organs and cell types is **$3.72*10^{13}$.** This is equivalent of having approximately 5 billion to **200 million trillion** cells. We can go on infinitely describing other creatures or any other living insects on earth. They have all been perfectly made at the right time, place and for a specific objective.

For example, research has shown that honeybees are a key factor in the pollination of roughly 100 corps. Surprisingly, a number of crops would almost become extinct if Honeybees didn't exit. Let's consider spending our Thanksgivings, for instance without sweet potatoes or pumpkin pie or even an orange. That sounds catastrophic in case there is absolutely no replacement at all.

Consequently, our lives on earth is never **an accident** because there is a reason behind every single human birth. For instance, an angel's function is to never stop praying: **"Holy, holy, holy is the Lord God Almighty, who was, and is, and is to come."** (Revelation 4:8). So their **purpose** is to continuously exalt His name and worship Him.

Now, let's consider the following situations:

1. Within hours of our birth, we could instantly **familiarize** ourselves with mom's voice or even dad's one. Later on, we may cry for some time because of having wet diaper, being hungry, feeling sleepy, not having been held by either one of our parents during the entire day or being sick. Such incidents may prompt them to perform the following actions:

- Immediately change our diaper and apply a suitable baby cream
- Provide us with a regular meal
- Walk and carry the baby gently while we will be singing some lullaby simultaneously
- Have their fingers run our back while holding our tommy upside down on their laps

1. Newly married couples with toddlers have become quite **occupied with their jobs**. Unfortunately, due to the world's constant unstable economy, an entire household may be forced to work to barely survive. Actually, this may result in hiring a babysitter at home. A child-minder will temporarily replace a working mother providing a toddler with a **supposedly** a motherly love, emotions, and warmth. As a result, working parents will not lose their sense of security as long as their income is sufficient to maintain a modest portion of savings per month after covering all the basic expenses.
2. So far we have seen some practical examples of divergent **personality roles**. Let's go one step further by analyzing another challenging character required to run Orphanage institutions. There are more than **143 million children** considered orphans. There are many **uncounted** that live on the streets, in slums, on the trains and even among untreated sewage. Often orphans may be abandoned by their relatives resulting in a criminal life in order to survive.
3. Hence, whether somebody functions as a parent, nanny or a volunteer specialist, one is to encompass at least some **positive personality traits**. The previous two examples illustrate that responsibility usually arises from **trustworthiness** observed by other individuals who turn to be our relatives, friends or corporation's supervisors possibly. In other words, when your work, ethics and behaviour are all **consistent** and transparent, your immediate supervisor will praise you and **assign** you more tasks as a result.

However, achieving such assignments require an individual who is **goal-oriented**, dedicated and a visionary. Therefore, any kind of creature on earth has been given some purpose on this earth to accomplish. Babies are made for a reason likewise. **"Everyone who is called by My Name, and whom I have created for My Glory, Whom I have formed, even whom I have made."** (Isaiah 43:7).

As a matter of fact, our offspring's life purpose or getting to know their reason for their living can be easily accomplished with parents who will consistently have provided their infants with a very healthy child-rearing environment. For instance, married couples know that their newborn infants can **recognize familiar faces**, especially those they see every day. In fact, the first time they hear their mother's **voice**, they immediately **become accustomed to it**. In comparison with the voice, one week could pass by before their mother's smell recognition process kicks in.

Nevertheless, the natural development of babies' sound, voice, gestures and various personality traits will sometimes take longer than usual and may **eventually stagnate**. Such delay arises from an **unhappy relationship**, selfish parents, and indirect reflection to the kind of lifestyle our Mam and Dad had been **previously exposed** upon living with their own parents.

To begin with, frequent screaming, quarrelling, **not listening** to one another and waiting for a reason to completely explode at each other normally hurt our seemingly happy marriages. Secondly, **not forgiving** each other occurring rather frequently (later on) bring about temporary separation, which is **strongly responsible** for divorce. Is the latter an overstatement? Absolutely not!

Should we read the New York Times, the Toronto Sun or the Huffington Post? Will we get a definite answer? Well, we may have a 50% probability of reaching somewhere. In a nutshell, we are always using the **world's wisdom** to search for answers. **"Stop fooling yourselves. If you count yourself above average in intelligence, as judged by this world's standards, you had better put this all aside and be a fool rather than let it hold you back from the true wisdom from above."** (1 Corinthians 3:18).

Psychologically, being **implosive**, **moody** and impatient are all early signs of being intolerant and **insensitive** towards one another's personal character. Experiments have illustrated that at **3** months, babies can remember new images or toys presented to them one to **six days earlier**. Consequently, an unstable home with habitually querying will gradually convey a **shaken-family** image into your infant's memory.

Most of these images are naturally **manifested** throughout her/his behaviour as he/she grows up. So, once **9 months** have elapsed from a toddler's life, a baby can **remember** more specific information, such as imitating actions she/he seen as long as **a week before**. In other words, they have a kind of **temporary memory** as in any RAM unit in a microchip, but they don't remember most of their experiences. Moving forward, whenever babies reach between 14 and 18 months old, **long-term memory** of particular events begins developing.

For example, I could recall some kind of images when I was about **30 months' old**. I vividly remember once while we were staying at my grandfather's 50-year-old-rusty-painted walls for the summer, I suddenly approached his desk and my right-hand reached out to his second drawer searching curiously for something and nothing. Next, our neighbour's son, who was roughly a 27-month-old infant, his mother showed up for a brief visit.

Subsequently, while we were playing together, he swiftly left our playground and immediately tried to touch the same drawer. However, I just completely blocked him pushing him away. Surprisingly, out of all incidents, this **insignificant situation** has always been stuck in mind. Apparently, this sort of situation had only a temporary **undamaging side effect** on my character's development process. Afterwards, my mother and her friend continued chatting.

Conversely, one of the parents or both may sometimes use **unintentionally**, based on their own upbringing, unacceptable methods to calm their baby down. For example, I was once vacationing in Dubai, we decided to go visit one of the malls. Initially, while going up on the electric escalators, I and my wife glimpsed a couple **seemingly caught-up** with the general scenery in the mall. Then, we observed a father using his **loudest voice** ever (towards at the baby's ears) to calm him down after his infant had been crying out in pain. Despite the father first attempt, his son's crying **remerged far worse** until the mother lastly interfered.

Although the entire seen lasted for only less than **70 seconds**, there is enough room to analyze carefully what had happened together dear readers. Firstly, the parent's **cultural backgrounds** absolutely prevailed assuming they had been extremely entertained a few months earlier. Secondly, we wouldn't like to be in the parent's shoes and **judge** them accordingly. "**Why do you look at the speck of sawdust in your brother's eye and pay no attention to the plank in your own eye?**" (Matthew 7:3).

Next, it is safe to infer the parent didn't internally attempt to instantly ask **God for guidance**. The parent just allowed negative thoughts to dominate his response for that fraction of a second. "**Be alert and of sober mind. Your enemy the devil prowls around like a roaring lion looking for someone to devour.**" (1 Peter 5:8). Since such precise **67-second-moment** had been swiftly shaping up, his entire reaction symbolized someone who didn't have any kind of **purpose** or meaning in his life.

Therefore, this sort of incident will have a **permanent** and **damaging** psychological side effect on their baby's character development process over the long-term. Such toddler's dissatisfaction with his father's character is expressed through projecting his special feelings of anger, depression, jealousy, sudden loss of appetite, etc... **when he is freely** playing with other babies.

On one hand, raising a toddler well represents a great challenge for most newly married couple as the way they live their life may have a grave risk on the kind of character/personality their infant will become in the future as a result.

On the other hand, other parents who have understood their **own calling from the Lord**, firmly believe even when they have no words to say, their destiny has already been set up knowing the fact that they may face some difficulties. They are **aware that the Holy Spirit** who resides in them **continuously** provides them with the necessary strength to pray and study thoroughly His word. "**In the same way, the Spirit helps us in our weakness. We do not know what we ought to pray for, but the Spirit himself intercedes for us through wordless groans.**" (Romans 8:26).

For instance, my grandmother, who used to be a regular church attendant and a piano player on Sundays, had been waiting for so long for my parents to get me baptized, but they had been quite engaged in some other family issues. So she took me one day along and had me baptized in her church. Her **heart was filled with joy** as she watched me being dipped into the bowl filled up with Holy water and being prayed on. Although I was 2 years old, it took me **38 years** to be rescued and **redeemed from sin**.

So, does such a ceremony hold any kind of spiritual advantage for our lives? Well, it doesn't; it just represents a public image of a spiritual come back that has already transpired in the person being baptized, some people would like to reinforce their own figurative strength in their community; neighbours and relative acceptance.

Others just like my grandmother, they could recall only an authentic account of their feelings while being in the **presence of the Lord**. Their actions are driven by the **Holy Spirit**-inspired intentions. My grandmother wanted to please God out of **love of His presence** and being devoted to **Him**. Eventually the Lord answered her prayers for her grandchildren though it might not have been initially **requested in words at the beginning from her mouth**, but the **Holy Spirit has always known her heart intentions**.

Additional Commentary:

I was around 4 years old when my grandma passed away. My mother used to tell me of her mother's (Alexandra) weekly Sunday worship service in the church. Many years later, Alexandra's plea to the Lord revealed itself into my sister's life in her early forties receiving Christ's eternal freedom from sin's enslavement as well.

B. CHILDHOOD (4-12 YEARS OLD)

Providing children with a loving, sound, calm, cooperative, and sensitive nurturing environment is one of the parent's top priorities. Also, any boys' or girls' room is the place where they feel happy, amused, emotionally satisfied and self-confident. However, establishing proper boundaries, limitations and a kind of a reward system are essential in maintaining a balance among the following four strategic-life corners: parent's **love** for their offspring, their essential **needs**, **extra demands** and the **freedom of ideas-exchanged** between each other.

The first corner of the childhood development procedure is love. When newly-married couples continuously express unconditional sacrifice, patience, forgiveness and listening to one another during their first year, this effectively contributes to building slowly yet progressively a similar parents' character being easily **reflected** during their child's early years.

Love isn't just a word said for the sake of only uttering it out of our mouths. It should be felt deeply within our souls. **"Husbands, love your wives, just as Christ loved the church and gave himself up for her."** (Ephesians 5:25).

Strictly speaking, being married is sometimes regarded exclusively as a workout in bed where foreplay followed by love-making is undoubtedly the conventional norm. Genuinely, a Christian home reflects an image of the relationship **between Christ and the church**. In all honesty, I grew up in some kind of a Christian home.

Our home is made of only 4 family members. I am six years older than my sister, Judy. We are Armenian Catholics. Our last name used to be "Kadidian", but when our great-grand-father ran away from Turkey and immigrated to Syria after the 1915 Armenian Genocide, the name was changed to "Kadid". We successfully remained **Christians by name**.

I had a very caring, loving and generous parents. My dad used to work around 50-60 hours per week. He was a civil engineer and my mother had a French literature degree as well. She would teach lessons privately. During the week, dad would take us out with his car to visit our friend's places where we played cards, Atari games and sometimes hide and seek. Not only indoor activities were carried out, but also some outdoor activities. So, our friends and families would get together at someone's garden or yard or even in the park to enjoy some **grilling and cooking hangouts**.

At other times, whenever we got back from high school, mom would ask for our regular monthly family meeting taking place at the sitting room. It is the area where usually either one or both parents would be available or sometimes only my mother due to my dad's **hectic** work schedule. During that meeting, they used to spend some time advising us about important life matters. For instance, behaving in certain situations, choosing our friends and discussing the most common key questions **bombarding** our lives.

Having done that, our responsibilities towards our actions were clearly explained. They had also stressed that being honest, hardworking, and confident are three essential characteristics eventually leading to a marvelous and **prosperous** life style. They had a couple of times stressed the fact that being spiritual can somehow help us in this materialistic world. However, the true meaning of spirituality had **never** been explained to either myself or sister. It had always been part of a vague-dead vocabulary.

Although I had a wonderful, sensitive and big-hearted parents, I regularly had a couple of **nightmares** while sleeping. Honestly, I used to get up sweating in the middle of the night. I was suddenly seized with a feeling of fear manifesting its self in form of being **guilty** when I turned 11 years old. Such fear was the result of continuous **accusations** that hadn't been resolved. It was very ambiguous stemming from an **antagonistic** source.

Nonetheless, Judy has been a **blessing** to the whole family. "**A woman giving birth to a child has pain because her time has come; but when her baby is born she forgets the anguish because of her joy that a child is born into the world.** "(John 16:21). For example, once while our parents were out, we were playing together jumping up and down on the bed as if it were our favourite tambourine.

Shortly after that, Judy suddenly fell off the bed, and her head accidentally hit the small wardrobe's handle very close-by. A couple of seconds later, blood started coming out of her head. So, I rushed straight off to the sitting room from which I quickly grabbed the two napkin boxes, emptied them out, and then I placed them all over her injured part of her head.

That circumstance proves that I do **care** for her; it signifies a high level of commitment our family members have for each other. I seem to be tuned in to our household's sentimental needs. Paradoxically, I hadn't been able to fully enjoy **God's blessing** since the world's **chains** had already launched their psychological attacks of worrisome thereby locking me in. I couldn't relate to what was occurring in my life to real faith in Christ. I was a **lost sheep**.

Generally, the Lord always wants to teach His sheep about themselves through reading and analyzing the scriptures, our life struggles, revelations from the Holy Spirit, and our brothers and sisters. "It is written in the Prophets: **'They will all be taught by God.** **'Everyone who has heard the Father and learned from him comes to me."** (John 6:45).

It took 29 years of my life until I have fully comprehended the lesson learned about fear. God conveyed to me that the enemy had introduced it so I will end up eventually losing my self-confidence. So saving my sister's life temporarily removed that fright. Our jumping was responsible for the unfortunate accident. Even though the entire family had always been away from **Him**; He has never stopped guarding our family with **His** angels. **"Jesus Christ is the same yesterday and today and forever."** (Hebrews 13:8).

As fear continues to present its in different parts of our lives, it starts to build toxic thoughts **reinforcing** our **negative** (natural) thinking brain cells. Such a process may ultimately result in an extremely unbalanced and emotional personality. In other words, you may observe in life certain individuals who may be **very enthusiastic** and happy on one hand. On the contrary, they can be capable of being **unreasonably depressed**.

Having an abrupt sense of humour, motivation and overconfidence represent the former. The latter can manifest itself through unpredictable and uncontrolled behavioural characteristic contributing to essentially a feature of the **Borderline Personality Disorder**. It is characterized by a noticeable form with **unstable** personal relationships, self-image and being extremely naïve at times.

For instance, once during one of those winter days, I would be home by 1:30 p.m. from my 3rd grade school. Then, I used to greet my mother. However, I ended up insulting her calling her some disrespectful names. So, my dad had me sallow some red pepper powder into my mouth. My action towards her wasn't at all intentional. I just behaved abnormally without any kind of **explanations**.

The second corner of the childhood development agenda is planning how basic necessities are decently maintained. They are constituted of four fundamental needs succeeded by minor others: residence, food, clothing, education, giving to others, savings for the future, etc… For example, spending too much money on brand names and leaving other basic requirements untouched gives the wrong impression for children. Their priorities will be **almost identical** to their parents' shopping habits.

Another necessary principal is that whenever our teen's behavior shows signs of improvement, rewarding them with some repeated mini-gifts is absolutely paramount. Regardless of its value, an unexpected present helps them analyze their psychological misconceptions about life's decisions. It raises their level of motivation **moving forward** without giving up and never stepping back.

Indeed, my mother and I had the chance to visit France when I almost turned 11 years old. My uncle had almost completed his French studies in literature in Paris-Sorbonne University. He had invited us over there. We had an amazing time as we toured discovering his on-campus university residence, the Louver, Eiffel Tower and Shanzelize.

While were looking over Paris from the Eiffel Tower, I was running around the area where they had been offering some antiques for sale. For some odd reason, an artistically small camera, which had been placed among other antiques, grabbed my attention. Surprising, I reached over there and **innocently got hold** of it and began pressing its buttons.

At that time, my mother was occupied with my uncle listening to one of the tour guides. A few moments later, we decided to move forward; however, the security alarm rang across the Towel, and the police instantly arrived. Having had the cops explained what they had seen through the hidden cameras, my mother apologized for them explaining that I didn't have the intention of taking that antique and handed it over.

Following this, we existed the Eiffel's tower police station heading back for the residence's restaurant. While we were talking, I just quickly stopped next to an ice-cream store on the spur of the moment and asked for a chocolate ice cream and some candies. Nonetheless, my uncle suggested that we were having lunch soon. Craving for it, I insisted, but he declined and my mother agreed. Truthfully, she whispered in my ears, "listen my dear, if you buy some sweets, you will not be enjoying as much your lunch meal as usual". This demand can be categorized as **an extra-unnecessary desire**.

According to the <u>Illustration picture</u> attached on the next page, a **limitation** on my wants had been placed by my uncle. Otherwise, this will provoke a huge pressure on the half circle which is supposed to encompass only our **parent's love** under normal spiritual circumstances lead by the Holy Spirit. The diagram further illustrates that once our extra need is gratified by them; the half circle boundary has been **violated**.

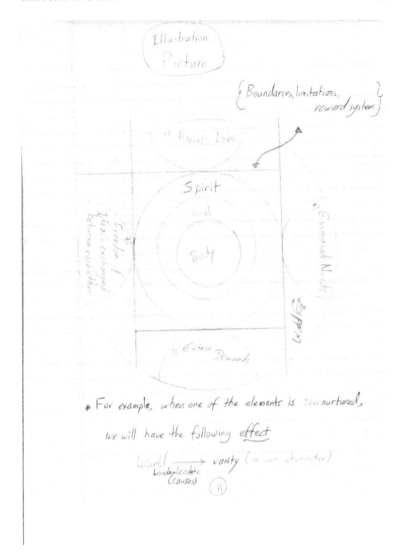

The urge now to provide an extra space in which to accommodate that wish is **real**. After that, the half-circle's edges will inflate and **expand** steadily until it **touches the soul** part of children. It consists of three parts: **brain** (the part of our body which processes information), **will** and **emotions**. (The circle **sidesteps** the spirit's part since I have never been **made aware** about the Holy Spirit; I would have learned about

God's presence if I had been attending the after-regular -Sunday-worship school teaching).

Consecutively, our children's brain, comprehends that their wish has been **granted signifying** the possibility of another one too. The next procedure is that we are always willing to focus on our children's **personal needs** before teaching them about Jesus's way of life. Eventually, their emotions have become extremely satisfied and unbalanced. This is the reason why we observe some children crying abnormally and loudly whenever their parents refuse to buy some stuff.

Instead, they need to have advised them and allowed for a free exchange of ideas to clarify the consequences of their actions. "**Fathers, do not exasperate your children; instead, bring them up in the training and instruction of the Lord."** (Ephesians 6:4)

Alternatively, a mixture of not imparting on that subject and enlightening our little ones will both accelerate and nurture the selfishness feeling in their minds. Having realized their requests are effortlessly achieved, they have the determination now to utilize their emotions in respect with cashing in on them. Additionally, to the abundant sources of information or pictures disclosed from music, movies, internet websites and friends, appropriate check is indispensable on what kind of message our preteens habitually receive.

Like listening to all sorts of songs, particularly the ones which portray love as a tool to invoke feelings of sexual intimacy demands parental supervision, such touching and fooling around with either women or men private parts. One way is to inspect their rooms from time to time possessing any suspicious materials while they are out for a while.

As a matter of fact, regardless of the gender, those preteens who become vulnerable to aggressive TV culture, their behavior could manifest their dissatisfaction with their own confused self-image in joining gang members. Alarmingly, a very few of them not only turn into drugs' addiction, but also begin to follow criminals or even serial killers' activities in extreme cases.

Therefore, a sufficient parent-children interchange of ideas without forcing our opinions is strongly advised along with teaching them how to differentiate between an unacceptable content of lyrics encompassing the "F", "B" and "Son of B" slangs and the acceptable ones. Another healthy approach is never throwing any kind of accusations; otherwise, such blaming will eventually foster an irreversible interest in a 12-year-old which becomes a stronghold during their early adolescence.

In the long run, the child becomes a brat severely attached to the **world** and his/her own flesh. **"For if you live according to the flesh, you will die; but if by the Spirit you put to death the misdeeds of the body, you will live."** (Romans 8:13).

Despite a society's pressure and couple's busy work schedule, releasing a boy or a girl's zest level can be attained by having them join any kind of physical activity offered at school. Some highs schools offer beginner classes as early as five years old for teaching a musical instrument, ballet, karate, swimming, basketball, etc...

Even being a regular active participant of a church choir is a great method for spiritual training. **"Let the message of Christ dwell among you richly as you teach and admonish one another with all wisdom through psalms, hymns, and songs from the Spirit, singing to God with gratitude in your hearts."** (Colossians 3:16)

C. ADOLESCENCE (13-17 YEARS OLD)

Being a civil engineer, my father used to spend roughly an extra 10-15 hours on construction sites added on his ordinary-40-hour weekly job task. Furthermore, the number of additional hours can extremely jump in case some constructions' workers building around their site get an unexpected sun stroke.

Remarkably, my mother took care of arranging for my 13-year-old birthday party. Expecting him not be present, he phoned from the firm's premises apologizing for not coming for my birthday. Actually, he returned home the same day at 1:30 a.m. after I had turned 13 years old.

Frankly speaking, I had never been keen on birthday celebrations (as my some of my close friends). The key factors in **developing our own self-image** classified as being either internal or external or both are:

- Our relationship with **God is mostly stimulated** by our parents
- The ability to maintain a sound relationship with our relatives and friends besides our parents
- The Comprehensive progression of the **Intellectual** process through the decision making process
- Understanding our emotional feelings **awareness**
- The psychological growth indicating the **consequences** of our actions
- Our natural biological development

To being with, our parents love to each other expressed via gestures, words and hugs, taking place in front of their teens, assist positively in flourishing the same human quality in our teens. Married people who first express their true, pure and never changing love for Christ before really committing themselves to one another usually **experience** the real faith. "**For we live by faith, not by sight.** (II Corinthians 5:7).

As a result, they will educate, train and share their faith with their adolescents accordingly. Christ continuously gives them strength to let their personal **selfish** needs be put aside as well. In this way, an appropriate transformation from the childhood phase to the adolescent phase is accomplished.

Whenever our parents let go of their **worldly** desires, they will sense beforehand bearable, but a very tough **resistance** from their minds which is part of their soul (as I had explained earlier in our childhood phase). The devil is responsible for provoking such mind instability since he knows the troublesome details of our past. **"For he has rescued us from the dominion of darkness and brought us into the kingdom of the Son he loves,"** (Colossians 1:13).

He could overhear our conversations with other people and ourselves. Nonetheless, He cannot be present everywhere like the Lord almighty; he banks on his other fallen angels to gather information.

Most importantly, he can neither know anything about our future or even predict with being 0.0000001% accurate. "**Who then is like me? Let him proclaim it. Let him declare and lay out before me what has happened since I established my ancient people, and what is yet to come**—yes, let them foretell what will come." (Isaiah 44:7).

For instance, suppose the family monthly income of a five-member family is $5000 living as expats in one of GCC countries. Let's assume for now that only one parent is working regardless of the gender. She/He decides not to register his/her children in one of the private schools since it may cost up to 6000 US yearly. Finding another one at half price with low quality of education is embraced instead. At the meantime, both parents have just spent $4000 buying the latest mobile phones, and clothes that are mostly brand names.

A devilish thought said, "Wow such schools are extremely expensive! Your savings will be wiped out". So, firstly the **idea** successfully **penetrates** our brain with a better possible solution, which is a **lie**. Next it feeds this deceit by forming part of a new decision to be made. Jesus said this of the devil: "**You belong to your father, the devil, and you want to carry out your father's desires. He was a murderer from the beginning, not holding to the truth, for there is no truth in him. When he lies, he speaks his native language, for he is a liar and the father of lies.**" (John 8:44).

That earlier scenario was brought about by the devil using some past particularities of the parent's history to his advantage. It might have been that the previous parent's father or mother did the same thing a long-time ago. Thus, such action will assuredly have a serious negative impact on forming an adolescent normal scholastic ability as 50% of the government curriculum in schools in such countries is well below standards compared with other countries. It is based on memorization instead of understanding the main materials' concepts.

In turn, the aftermath of graduating has a huge amount of influence over her/his social, emotional intellectual expansion process, still the physical process is an independent internal character based on our normal biological growth. For example, students who have matured in such educational surroundings are generally regarded as being timid and fearful.

So, most private academies or institutions in such countries can usually make up for the loss in the quality of education and the integrity of forming an adolescent normal identity specifically in this region.

If the household income is sufficient, they must show full responsibility by educating them competently as it is a <u>required part of their faith</u>. **"For we must all appear before the judgment seat of Christ, so that each of us may receive what is due us for the things done while in the body, whether good or bad."** (<u>II Corinthians 5:10</u>).

In spite of receiving the free gift of eternal life, all believers have to submit a comprehensive **narrative of their way of living**. Followers of Christ aren't excused from adhering to God's law. Our creator desires to know whether we have successfully contributed to properly guiding our youth with **practical Holy-Spirit-guided** solutions during their education's battlefield years under our stewardship. He has absolute ownership of the world in which we earn a living. Our **finance's accountability must follow His will** in our lives.

Otherwise, we have chosen to act as thieves **crushing our youngster's hopes** once they have become adults. Do we need to store plenty of dollars in the bank on the expense of hindering our adolescents basic right of getting the right education? When we have real faith, our thoughts, wishes feelings and actions will be normally and automatically <u>aligning themselves with Him</u>.

Then, the Lord will be undoubtedly our first priority with no exceptions at all as such, money, clothing, worries of tomorrow, surviving and everything else become so trivial. Jesus has assured us of providing with all our lives' necessities. **"But seek first his kingdom and his righteousness, and all these things will be given to you as well."** (Matthew 6:33).

However, if parents were living in communities where they had access to multiple options, they would choose the most reasonable one. For instance, some free state schools in the United States or provincial ones in Canada charge only for books verses those private ones which their tuition my skyrocket up to $10,000 annually. Since both provide the same syllable, choosing the state/ provincial ones could be wiser to save up that substantial sum of money later during their university years.

Others believe it is up to their adolescents to do well in school regardless of the quality of education they usually get in. In addition, they are firmly convinced as their grown-ups know the subject of the study, they can do very well wherever they are. Some outstanding ones are ironically successful businessmen, Doctors, scientists, etc...On the flipside, some are failures perceived well and defined by the world, but what is the reason? Who is to blame?? Maintaining a **balance** between focusing on our own career and having a **continuous spiritual growth with Christ** are key elements to receiving guidance from the Holy Spirit to climb up the career ladder.

So, a high school's circle of friends and its surrounding environment support our younger's social development procedures. An excellent school has periodical meetings with parents to report the kind of activities in which they are involved. Some extra-curricular activities are participation in competition with other schools, voicing your opinion regarding changing the curriculum and recommending hands on in-class practical training with certain literature and science subjects.

Self-confidence, observing other students' personalities, discovering their own strong and weak points and being self-committed are some preliminary transferrable social attitudes which also enhance a balanced and an affectionate teenager personality, which had been formerly brought about by our parent's declaring that **God** is solely loved more than the world. **"Do not love the world or anything in the world. If anyone loves the world, love for the Father is not in them."** (1 John 2:15).

Fourthly, of all the ingredients composing youngster's own identity, the emotional evolvement mechanism is vital in analyzing how the first three points precisely affect our teen's emotional reactions such as, love, hate, sadness, etc... As a result, **a greater understanding of their common paradoxical conduct is materialized**.

For instance, during the time, our family was vacationing in Athens, Greece, we once stopped at a restaurant where we had some Greek appetizers such as, Taramosalata, Tzatziki and Loukaniko. A Greek dish starter mainly consists of Fish roe, breadcrumbs, a filo pastry pie of Spinach and feta cheese, olive oil, lemon juice, yogurt, cucumber, garlic, etc... Not only their vegetable mix is very authentic, but also their music. They usually have a 5-member band playing some of their old music being synchronized with food eating process.

Meanwhile, I and Judy left the terrace and sat next to a telephone kiosk though we had been notified many times not to leave our family's table. We just wanted to watch the various sorts of street activities closed-by. There was some painting, drums playing and a couple of comedians who had an exquisite sense of timing.

As a matter of fact, the external sources of information --> Availability of entertainment --> gave rise to a new level of knowledge --> interpreted by the brain --> followed by an action: willingness to walk out of our boundaries --> as soon we saw the activities --> feelings of happiness, laughing and excitement were provoked as a result. This is a decision making process defined **as being active.**

Conversely, **readiness to execute something without being pressured from our intellectual course is characterized by being passive.** We sometimes love making **spontaneous decisions.** For example, Bournemouth is another city I have been to. It has a total population of over 400,000. Indeed, their general populace appreciates having one of the most enjoyable climates in the UK with mild temperatures and lengthy sunny days.

Furthermore, it is situated next to a beach where more than 5 million tourists travel yearlong. Staying over there for almost 40 days was my father's idea. He said, "when you roam around another country in a divergent content for some time, you will definitely learn about a new culture, you may feel a certain level of excitement and adventure, getting away from us may help you assert your independence, I guess Um... and making new friends... Um is another great cause."

Was really distancing myself from my parents a major contributor to my independent psychological growth?!!**Undisguised affection, more time spent with friends, antagonistic behavior are some preconceived emotional decisions.** Apathetic form of listening is called reactive listening. As we grow during our teens, we tend to **listen to ourselves and ignore others.**

Once I was sitting on a bench waiting for the next bus stop in Bournemouth, an elderly suddenly showed up and started conversing nonstop. I swiftly managed to pay attention for the first 15 minutes, but I just lost concentration and interest and kept on saying yes. In any case, feelings of boredom and our **self-fulling prophecy** softly whispers, **"There is nothing I can do." That is the way I am."**

As a result, we begin acting directly **from emotions seeking first to be understood** instead of the other way around. Automatic nonsense discussion and pride are products of such brain-flourishing and absorbed knowledge. **"Nor should there be obscenity, foolish talk or coarse joking, which are out of place, but rather thanksgiving."** (Ephesians 5:4).

I had mentioned in the previous childhood stage that when we become young adults, our human character mimics exactly our parents. Alarmingly, some initial signs of youth's unkind and **arrogant reactions may start as being insignificant in their lives**; they will be probably carried over and manifested in their 30s.

Substantiating the above mentioned, I encountered a serious situation with the host family with whom I was supposed to sojourn for 2 months in the summer. The roommate with whom I was sharing the room used to wake up in the middle of the night and talk to himself. He was so annoying that I couldn't get enough sleep during the night. Despite advising the host family, the same disturbance continued nonstop.

In reality, my mother used to call me twice a week checking whether I was really enjoying my stay over there. Incredibly she phoned once and said, "I have had a strong feeling you aren't comfortable, you need to keep us updated." So, I informed her about the matter. So, she suggested talking with the school manager. Later on, I brought up the issue, but he was inattentive with harsh words. He was an example of someone who **was presumptuous.** Some other students added, "our director has an eccentric personality, we never know when he is happy." He was in his late 40s.

Hence my dad ended up flying to Bournemouth to address the situation with the academic director of the college. He was responsible for at least 200 students and more than 30 teachers. I was immediately moved to a much better host family who had really listened to my needs for the entire remaining period. Besides, I was given a spacious single room. There were other students who were given single rooms as well. Mom's sincere caring about my situation indirectly resulted in turning the manager's decision with the utmost care. "**Turning your ear to wisdom and applying your heart to understanding.**" (Proverbs 2:2).

The 5th cause stirring our make-up is the direction our juniors' cognitive advancement spill over into our lives. E.g. insecure parents who have been just coping with their own heartbreaking conditions fail to act quickly during a family emergency. In other words, their **past has never been resolved**. It always manifests itself as a monster called depression relating to their defeated-unresolved (**moving forward**), forgiveness-locked (**removing guilt**) and fear-driven (**perfect love**) soul. That is why they can't contribute positively to reducing their own children's emotional suffering.

Dramatically, any kind of personality traits' adjustments discharged by their youngster can't be figured out. So, any treatment techniques may be used, such as yelling, screaming, nocking, uttering filthy language or malicious words and list goes on. Such parents have usually released their own frustrations dumping on their younger's generation's early years a permanent deep psychological scar.

However, God can release us from our burdens. **"Come to me, all you who are weary and burdened, and I will give you rest."** (Matthew 11:28). In comparison with His (God) way-out, man-made creative solutions suggested by having faith in our own will and determination may lessen the amount of anxiety, phobias, fears from life circumstances. Some other researchers believe that practicing some kind of mediation by being alone somewhere in a mountain or at home contribute directly to confronting an individual with his own failures.

In my opinion, I partially agree with the introspection methodology; can it really help us out? Is the world capable of saving us from an extremely diabolical state-of-the-art bleakness? Have we considered all the ramifications? Well, according to an independent study, 80% of individuals who pursue therapy for depression are treated successfully. Whereas %15 of those **psychologically tormenting** themselves die by suicide. Alarmingly, it is the **second-most popular** cause of death for young people 15-24 years old. Also, the rates for those who are divorced or widowed are the topmost.

In addition, recent research seems to corroborate some interesting facts about desperation:

- **Depression** is predicted to rise to second place in 2020 in UK alone
- About a quarter of the world population will experience some kind of mental health problem in the course of a year, with mixed anxiety and desolation
- Women are more likely to have been treated for a mental health problem than men, and about ten percent of children experience the same issue at any one time
- **Dispiritedness** affects 1 in 5 older people worldwide

We can say it is apparent that other people **desperately need serious assistance**. Once more, people believe that relying on the world or their own strengths is the solution. They may go through counselling and simultaneously decide to join gym, a dance class or a martial art one.

After all, but he said to me, "**My grace is sufficient for you, for my power is made perfect in weakness.**" Therefore, I will boast all the more gladly about my weaknesses, so that Christ's power may rest on me." (2 Corinthians 12:9). Most of those **quick fix** scenarios provide a **temporary** relief for our unsettled psychological controversies. They don't deal directly with their **original roots** of living in continuous panic, guilt and an agonizing breakdown. Instead, they would rather **suppress** them for years.

I remember once while I was waiting for my flight from Ataturk Airport in Istanbul departing for London. I saw two men in their mid-30s. At the beginning, they were actually laughing uncontrollably, and they were very loud. Notably, they drank one bottle of Jonnie Walker each straight from the bottle in a period of less than 20 minutes.

Their heads were moving sideways, and almost their bodies were collapsing on the floor.

Having addictions for work, food, alcohol or sex commonly results in family separation, obesity, physical abuse and unfaithfulness. Such individuals ignore **their inner spirit calling** for changes in their personality to become adaptable with any kind of **circumstances according to God's Will. Those changes stem from the Holy Spirit who becomes present in our spirit once we are born again.**

Our spirit is composed of **our hunch, togetherness with God and conscience**. Alternatively, our heart contains our **thought process, determination to do something, emotions and the conscience** element only. Our hunch is **the Lord's inner voice speaking with us**, so it is critical that we both hear and listen to **Him**.

A fellowship with God involve four essential characteristics: absolutely trusting God regardless of the circumstances, being overwhelmed by **His Grace**, living our lives in unconditional truth and without any sin, and not associating ourselves unfaithful persons. However, we can sit down with them, and let them know about our faith without being drawn into either their lifestyle or character.

In plain English, actions including praying, fasting, checking up on your fellow brothers or sisters, etc... are great **examples of being very close to God's nature**. The essence of His nature is justice too so free will has been given to everyone **with no favoritism**. Our conscience is our **capacity to choose right from wrong based on our own morals and principals**. On one hand, it may make us realize that we have just committed an inappropriate action.

On the contrary, if we become irrational and careless of selecting any choice in our lives, we have disregarded the adverse, physical, mental and spiritual-long-term side effects. For example, when the Pharaoh refused to accept Moses's message advocating a wrong action against God, his **real conscience gradually didn't bother him**. Later on, **he invented his own one. His God symbolized a Genie ready to satisfy his endless dreams available at a click of a mouse.**

Let's analyze his heart, he is known for his **arrogance --> his ego overpowers his thought** process --> he will be willing to make a decision exclusively satisfying his self-glorified image underlining his recurring emotional satisfaction. This means his conscience part of his spirit has **been bypassed** and doubtlessly ignored filled up with **self-pettiness**.

"**Why do you harden your hearts as the Egyptians and Pharaoh did? When Israel's god dealt harshly with them, did they not send the Israelites out so they could go on their way?**" (1 Samuel 6:6). The more stubborn he became (the person's conscience is freezed or dead), his personal judgement turned into his man-made-close-circle decision **from the thought process.**

Sin will eventually permanently **separate** ourselves from God because we are validating a wrong action as what had happened with Moses. **Our hearts will harden** every time we hear someone speaks about the bible and our hearts stay the same.

Unless we develop and maintain a clear (1) **conscience** during our childhood, it will be **buried** and our **intimacy with the Lord** will be totally replaced by our old-sinful nature. "**Dear friends, if our hearts do not condemn us, we have confidence before God**" (1 John 3:21).

We will continually live in a vicious psychological circle of (1) **immorality**. Our hearts have become accustomed to cheating or any kind of sin; it turns into a **contaminated** container full of lives' hardships, depression, discontent, jealousy, dishonesty, wickedness, blasphemy, etc...

This causes us to either temporarily or permanently (2) **block the Lord's revelation process** --> the Holy Spirit is saddened. At the end, the very (3) **warm relationship** we used to have with God through praying and fasting is broken. **Our heart refuses to listen to Him.** Eventually, it will (4) **harden** and almost completely shut down.

Let's revisit the heart formula. So, a person's heart/Pharaoh now contains her/his thought process, determination to do something, emotions only **with no** conscience.

Decisions made by the heart = An individual's Soul (thought process + determination to do something + emotions)

"**See to it, brothers and sisters, that none of you has a sinful, unbelieving heart that turns away from the living God. But** encourage one another daily, as long as it is called "Today," so that none of you may be hardened by sin's deceitfulness." (Hebrews 3:12-13).

THE UNIVERSITY OF KANSAS

THE UNIVERSITY OF KANSAS
Office of Foreign Student Services
Lawrence, Kansas 66045-1978
(913) 864-3617

WELCOME TO THE UNIVERSITY OF KANSAS

We have prepared the following materials to help you in your journey and transition to Kansas. As you prepare to depart for the United States there is some basic information which is important for you to know. We invite you to read the enclosed information carefully. Hopefully, it will answer most of the questions you might have.

WHAT TO PREPARE! As you can tell from the map, we are located in the geographical center of the contiguous United States. Being in the middle of the country, we have four definite seasons. At the time of your arrival for fall semester, the weather should still be hot. Daytime temperatures will average from approximately 32 to 36 degrees C. It will become cooler during September and October and winter temperatures in December and January can reach -18 C. Unless you plan to buy winter clothing here, you should plan a wardrobe for the changing seasons. In addition to clothing, you should bring at least two months supply of any medications you may need. Prescriptions for medicines, eyeglasses, medical records, immunization record, etc. should be translated into English. Medical costs in the U.S. are very expensive and health insurance is the only way to protect yourself from financial disaster if you are seriously ill or injured. If you cannot obtain health insurance before you come to the University of Kansas (KU), you should plan to enroll in one of the available insurance programs immediately upon arrival. If you would like to send some of your belongings in advance, you may address them to our office. You may also use our address for receiving mail until you have an address of your own here. We will receive your packages and mail and store them until you arrive. Money you bring with you should be in traveller's checks. (It is easy to underestimate the amount of money necessary for the first month you will be here. You should bring as much with you as you can.) Money sent to the University can be by bank draft or check made out to you and the University of Kansas. If bank drafts or checks made out to the University are in excess of funds necessary for tuition and fees, the excess amount will be returned to you at the time of enrollment.

WHEN YOU ARRIVE IN KANSAS CITY, you will be within 50 miles of Lawrence. There is a regular shuttle service between the airport (KCI) and Lawrence. Shuttle service will cost about $20.00. If you have already sent a contract for student housing, or you intend to live on-campus and you arrive between August 13 and August 18, you should go to Joseph R. Pearson Hall (JRP), 1122 West Campus Road. There will be temporary housing available there. Students with contracts for Jayhawker Towers or Stouffer Place can go directly to those locations. If you have no housing contract and intend to live off-campus, you can go to one of the motels on the list until you can find an apartment or other off-campus accommodation. ONCE YOU ARE IN LAWRENCE, FINDING A PLACE TO LIVE SHOULD BE YOUR FIRST CONCERN. Students who do _not_ participate in the *International Student Services New Student Orientation Program* should plan on attending *one* of the two general informational meetings scheduled for *either* Thursday, August 15 from 2-4 p.m. *or* Saturday, August 17 from 2-4 p.m. Both meetings will be in Room 330, Strong Hall. Bring to that meeting: your passport, I-20 or IAP-66 form, and I-94 card (the small white card issued when you enter the United States). Students who are participating in the *Orientation Program* should follow the instructions stated on the registration form. We will have additional information ready for you in the *Orientation Program* and in the general meeting.

WE HOPE YOUR JOURNEY TO KANSAS IS A PLEASANT ONE

Main Campus, Lawrence
College of Health Sciences and Hospital, Kansas City and Wichita

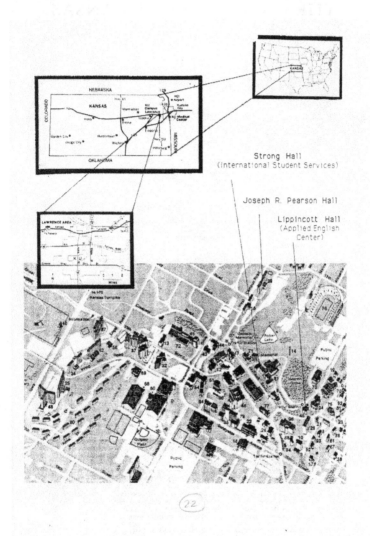

Writing old computer programming language such as Pascal was one of my favorite hobbies. I used to spend many hours per week writing small programs which included some arithmetic operations. My own interest in computing inspired my father so much that he began thinking about some additional university options.

Having scored 93% in the overall GPA in grade 12, strongly reaffirmed dad's determination that studying in the US was the best possible option available. However, my mother wasn't strongly convinced about the states. She preferred doing the undergraduate studies in some reputable university. Afterwards, I could complete my higher studies anywhere based on my marks.

Regardless of her opinion, he proceeded with submitting my high school transcripts to more than 70 American universities. The majority of them were state ones and others were private institutions but recognizable around the world. Three months later, of the offers he had received; he liked very much the University of Kansas because it had a huge campus holding roughly 30,000 students.

Their Academic and administrative staff accounted for almost 13,000 as well. It was opened in 1866 encompassing the largest and oldest public university in the U.S. State of Kansas, yet my mother hadn't at all brought into such idea. It is known as a public research university. Dad was certainly excited about me being accepted into KU as it would represent a turning point in his son's life. Simultaneously, it was the second milestone in my life. He would ask around his friends about the plan he had for my future. They may have agreed with him at the first place, but my mother wasn't convinced.

"Plans fail for lack of counsel, but with many advisers they succeed." (proverbs 15:22). Not only counselling others – prior to taking an action on a family's break through choice – is definitely necessary, but also wholly releasing our offspring's future to **God's will** is of paramount importance. When parents let Him take control of directing their spirituality driven plans (by **belief** only), **this indicates that they have strong faith in the unseen.**

"By faith Moses' parents hid him for three months after he was born, because they saw he was no ordinary child, and they were not afraid of the king's edict." (Hebrews 11:23). Moses parents had always had a firm conviction that the Lord kept a lookout for any kind of danger that their baby might constantly face.

My father certainly wanted the best for my future; however, **he used his own wisdom relying completely on his own life's experience** and didn't know any better, yet God has always had other plans for us; He unquenchably tries to get into our **hearts**. I love and respect my parents because they have worked so hard on bringing me up to the kind of man I have become.

Again, the Lord always finds a way to save us (redeem us from our sins). **"God did this so that they would seek him and perhaps reach out for him and find him, though he is not far from any one of us."** (Acts 17:27). I remember that just few months before my departure to the states, we used to have a bi-weekly ordinary visit from a friend of my parents. **(1)** He had accepted Jesus as his saver just before meeting us. *(numbers 1...9 counts how many times God tried to reach out to me).*

In spite of being delighted to share his story with my family, I wasn't at all paying any attention to his testimony. I was a little more than 17 years old at the time. Watching movies about celebrities, listening to the Bee Gees, being fascinated by, Hulk Hogan, who was a 12-time WWF/WWE World Heavyweight Champion and hearing the song titled, "Hotel California" were my idols.

Besides being utterly absorbed by the opening patterns of the new era of the high tech age, the British scientist Tim Berners-Lee had introduced the World Wide Web by the end of 1989. Concurrently, older forms of media have become out-of-date as the information era began to penetrate every single part of our lives. Unless parents adequately enlighten their grown-ups about the pros and cons of the internet usage, it will steadily take over their thought process and educational life style.

Countless hours may be spent in front of the Web being exposed to a variety of different acceptable and inappropriate materials. Eventually, we will have internationally embraced this technology as another form of an icon which may drift us away from the Lord. **"Formerly, when** you did not know God, you were slaves to those who by nature are not gods." (Galatians 4:8). We would rather entertain our selfish-egotistical desires being controlled by earthly gadgets.

Similarly, when analyzing some events that took place in the Old Testament, we can observe people used to be busy getting married, buying homes, establishing new forms of businesses and even kings occupying other lands. All such events had turned them away from God precisely mimicking present-day stories. **"For in the days before the flood, people were eating and drinking, marrying and giving in marriage, up to the day Noah entered the ark."** (Matthew 24:38).

Clearly and transparently understanding God's will or plan in our lives is crucial before agreeing on a family decision. It may cause an unexpected outcome not as we initially planned.

Ranked the third of my grade-12 class, I felt quite confident with my own capabilities. I really wanted to leave home, but images of growing up as a little kid came across. On the other hand, the entire family participated in preparing my luggage. Loading and unloading the baggage and some other stuff in dad's car were my chores.

During the time the vehicle began moving slowly (only in my mind), I looked through its window town spotting as if it had been my first time ever visiting my hometown. Once we arrived to the airport, we checked-in our bags, but there was an announcement about a delay in the plane's departures schedule. We eventually had to stay an extra 4 hours.

In spite of the **4-hour lateness signaling God's first warning**, we got on the plane, and it shortly took off. Thirty minutes later, a weird smell of one of its gas wings began and persisted; the pilot kept flying above the clouds circularly fixed to a certain position in the air. This continued for the next 45 minutes until the passengers were informed of a prior gas leakage. Actually, it was so severe that any small error might have caused the gas to be in a direct contact with some other exterior and inflammable aircraft elements resulting in a possible wing explosion.

Some passengers began praying while others were sleeping, and the third group cared about nothing. They were only concerned about chitchatting. Next, my mother reemphasized her point that we shouldn't have travelled anyways. She almost had a panic attack; meanwhile, a couple of air hostesses were once again demonstrating airbag's conventional use in case of an emergency landing. The pilot immediately began descending very slowly with the least amount of gas leakage.

He took a step after making sure that any kind of electrical risk had been cleared away since clouds began dispersing from each other. At last, by the time the plane peacefully landed on the runway with little gas left, a portion of the passengers had already vomited especially, the children and the elderly. **The Lord has just talked to us through technical problem (2)** against a decision we had made earlier revealing his dissatisfaction with our choice. I would like to reiterate that I began to lose a bit of **peace (A)** in my heart. Unexpected negative events in our lives usually trigger our depression back in action unless we ask Christ to take over our burdens. **"Come to me, all you who are weary and burdened, and I will give you rest."** (Matthew 11:28). *(letters A...F signifies the personalty traits being lost over time)*

After passing US customs, the family decided to stay in Best Western Hotel till I was permanently moved to KU's on campus-residence. It was within a walking distance from our stay. Next morning, we had our complimentary breakfast and strolled into town where the university rested on 1100 acres of land situated in Lawrence, Wichita, Overland Park, Salina, and Kansas City, Kansas, with the main campus located in Lawrence on Mount Oread, the highest location in Lawrence.

We had true feelings of contentment including my mother who started lightening up a bit after visiting some parts of the campus, especially the dormitories. The fact it was during the beginning of August, and it was greenish everywhere lessened her dissatisfaction with everything. In comparison with Lawrence, Montreal gets really hot up to 100 Degrees F and extremely humid.

Later on, we arrived to Jayhawker Towers welcomed by the manager. He happened to be in his sophomore year, which is equivalent to a student's second year of a study/course at a US college. I was born on January 15th, 1974. I was only 17 years and a half.

While we were touring the tours; he explained a list of general regulations of which he stressed the following ones: no alcohol is allowed in the dorms and on KU's owned land, smoking depends on your roommate; also, pets aren't allowed except for fish within an aquarium. Making our way along, we stopped by Tower D where I was introduced to David with whom I was living on campus.

While my parents felt they had undoubtedly completed most of the necessary check-ups starting with visiting the university, inspecting my residence including the dorm's cleanness, my cafeteria meal's plans and ending with its medical centre, they confirmed their flight reservations to Disney Land and flew within a week.

Waving goodbye to mother, father and sister, I just remained silent, for my heart was heavy and my soul was low. Shortly after their departure, there was once again an unexplained numbness in my feelings. At the same time, **taking my own responsibility for my own actions thrilled my free will.**

I mostly had a new strategy in respect with focusing solely on my undergraduate freshman curriculum. As in previous years, the **lord had been sidestepped as If had been the speaker bypassing a question posed by the audience by saying that it would take too long to answer it**.

With every stubborn and self-centred step, the Lord never abandons us. **He is almighty, Omnipotent and Omniscient.** He tries more and more to bring us deliverance because he knows our hearts. So, he placed a roommate who was a very devout Christian along my academic path endeavouring to save me. **"Search me, God, and know my heart; test me and know my anxious thoughts."** (Psalm 139:23).

Alternatively, this all depends on our openness to fully receiving **His message** well in our heart. Is Abboud believed to be inclined towards accepting the Lord's salvation message out of his own personal choice? It is the never-ending timing off which will be spiritually realized by all who have been saved, by who all who have been redeemed by the precious blood of Christ. The bible says, **"again he appoints a certain day, "Today saying through David so long afterward, in the words** already quoted, "Today, if you hear his voice, don't harden your hearts." (Hebrews 4:7).

(3) **David** who was from Indonesia majoring in mechanical engineering, and would always attend Sunday Service, suggested moving and showing up together at the Chapel, but sometimes I just didn't feel like going there, so he would make it alone. After a couple of times, he stopped inviting me because he felt I wasn't serious at all.

The Lord tried again to convey **His message through David who wanted to get a profitable spiritual harvest once I heard the word.** I represent the seed inspired by the Holy Spirit to direct him towards motivating and greatly encouraging me about God, with no avail.

Likewise, the bible says, "Listen then to what the parable of the sower means: When anyone hears the message about the kingdom and doesn't understand it, the evil one comes and snatches away what was sown in the heart. This is the seed sown along the path. "(Matthew 13:18). My heart was so hard the first time I heard His verses and hymns that they only lasted until the worship service was over. I symbolize the first category of nonbelievers.

Having settled my belongings in my room, I glanced through the **documentation of which some papers about KU's Orientation Program caught my attention**. The university generally determines certain fixed days for it at early September. I arrived at the end of August, 1991.

Since it was only offered for new comers, I decided to turn up to learn about the special programs, events, activities which permit foreign students to brush up on the American culture while sharing theirs on campus and surrounding communities. On that day, I made some friends, and I learnt about getting my student ID, using buses to travel within the campus, the campus recreational facilities and Jayhawks Basketball Team.

One of the communities attending the orientation had no name; it was more like an independent one as far I could remember. It had an office just right to the event's vicinity. So, **for some odd reason; I just walked in their place, and there were around 12 students.** Some of them were standing and chatting; others were just sitting. Suddenly, I humped to bump into (4) **Kim**; she was an 18-year-old chemistry major. I knew her name from the tag placed perpendicular to her shoulder. We had spoken almost an hour with respect to our educational backgrounds. She actually asked me, "are you interested in the bible group meetings?", "We have hymns as well". I said," Sure I am." A week later, she picked me early Sunday morning right in front of Tower D. While were conversing the car, she asked, "Have you had breakfast yet?" I replied, "No". She said. "We will all eat together then. "Next, I said," who else is coming? She answered, "**my brother** is on his way too."

Expecting to meet her brother, I was completely mistaken because it turned to be her fellow in Christ. We prayed before eating as I used to do with David. **Such practice was never done at home.** We had an interesting discussion being tolerant with other traditions. Next, we headed for off-campus where we arrived at an outdoor mass. There was a speaker right at the centre of the crowd. He was holding the bible while addressing the **Word of God very boldly.**

Likewise, I sat, listened and even started praising him slightly louder than usual. Nonetheless, the message evaporated up in the air the moment I left the congregation. Indeed, one of those days, I cancelled the gathering with Kim. Other times, **I just stayed in the dorms acting pessimistic and confused.**

Once I began shifting my attention away from the Lord, **normal feelings of (B) Joy** I used to have steadily but not totally left my soul. As I mentioned before, our soul has three elements: **mind, will and emotions.** The **devil manages to get through our minds by sending incorrect negative pieces of information.** For example, "<u>don't go to the meeting</u>", "there is nothing in it for you", "you had better concentrate on your studies", "you haven't changed at all". "Come on get angrier, answer your own parents back."

As for my first semester, the *AEC 057 Summer Special Studies in Advanced Writing* Course was a prerequisite for two of the second semester courses. That was the only writing course I passed with A- in 10 weeks instead of the regular-15-week one. I recall quite well spending some hours studying in one of the libraries on campus. Writing an essay which usually commences with a topic sentence and a controlling idea.

One on hand, I was very successful full-time student in my first year with a 3.7/4.00 G.P.A., but my social life suffered greatly except for the swimming elective course which I had shortly after my calculus II class in the second term at 9:00 a.m. weekly. Not having much friends and peer pressure **worsened my deep-silent depression. It was more like a sleeping bear.** Thinking about the quick fix, I decided to work 10 hours a week as a buss boy.

It was a great opportunity to meet other students who were working and attending KU simultaneously. Avoiding pre-marital sex, drugs and staying out of trouble within my social environment reinforced the idea of having a job. Nonetheless, I had a bit of time to go clubbing. It is sometimes the place where **students flex their muscles by consuming so much alcohol till they get drunk and eventually throw up.**

Once you let the smallest **bit of sin walk in your life, you have opened the door for it to grow bigger until it perfectly takes control of your life and indirectly and calmly destroys your life and character.** Hearing frequently about clubbing, I got so curious that I decided to go out one day and got drunk. On my way back, I felt quite dizzy with false sense of excitement. Upon arriving to Tower D, I went to the wrong floor and entered my keys. They were stuck and stopped moving in both directions. After several attempts, the student residing opened the door with normal greetings and used a special spray to discharge them.

Frankly speaking, I got up the next week with some drowsiness and body aches. Not to mention the embarrassing circumstance into which I got myself waking up a student at 3:30 a.m. was out of place. Ironically, **sharing incidents of being stupid, acting foolishly have been the most talked about topics among freshman students**. They usually entertain spiritually empty people. *What do you think about now?!!!!!*

Those are just a sample of the discussions I heard on August 1991. There are far more women –insulting words and experiences which have surprisingly been very popular around undergraduates' social environments. They genuinely feel pride in being futile. "Avoid godless chatter, because those who indulge in it will become more and more ungodly." (2 Timothy 2:16).

When we stumble over our vision and make an improper decision, it gives the **key** to devil to enter our minds, our lives will not become centred on the Lord. We will pay the consequences of our actions. A good example is just like what had happened to the Prophet Lot though he heed been known by God to be a righteous man; **he had made a wrong decision about living among sinners in Sodom. As a result, he ended up losing his wife and finally his two daughters.**

We need to build our lives based on **His priorities**. However, as I had been a non-believer, I am **outside His** protection from the Devil. **"Nor should there be obscenity, foolish talk or coarse joking, which are out of place, but rather thanksgiving."** (Ephesians 5:4).

Since the devil has got a very small opening through our minds, he will present his next suggestion via **activating hidden images stuck in our permanent memory since we have never had a real fellowship with the Lord**. I had mentioned earlier about being in Bournemouth, and how I changed residence. Another main reason was that I came across a couple of pornographic material left around my first host family's residence.

"The eye is the lamp of the body. If your eyes are healthy, your whole body will be full of light." (Matthew 6:22). To review, *an individual's heart=one's Soul (mind+will+emotion) + one's conscience*. Our **eyes** are the door to our hearts. **When we see those images for the first time, we either choose to close the magazines or continue looking.**

Selecting the letter option indicates such images have been successfully **filtered** through my (a) *mind* symbolizing psychological acceptance. My will further analyzes them by (b) **taking an action** to ask about the source. Next, I literally react being (c) **influenced by emotions to lastly buy** such magazine which represents the source.

We can infer that sin has **four different important attributes**: it has resulted from the (a) natural **corrupt nature** of the human being since (b) falling from heaven, voluntarily choosing evil by being (c) independent from God; such autonomy means we have become determined the devil to **(d) be our master**, and no one is excluded from committing a sin. Hence, **we have truly (insulted) the Lord since he is the source of permanent light** by attaching **darkness** to His Holy Nature.

Our sin (darkness) can never surpass **His boundaries** or even come close. "**Everyone who sins breaks the law; in fact, sin is lawlessness.** "(1 John 3:4). "**For it is from within, out of a person's heart, that evil thoughts come—sexual immorality, theft, murder,**" (Mark 7:21).

In the course of my sophomore year, I had 3 computer science courses of which two were programming ones and the third was theoretical. I had an elective one as well. I had a total of 4 courses enrolled on a full-time basis. I replaced a political science course by philosophy by the end of the first week of class. It was much more interesting and mathematically oriented.

I **was self-assured** to have a great success based on my prior year. While attending one of my classes, I met **(5) Christian fellow from Nigeria** with whom I went out a couple of times. He was actually involved either in the previous gospel group or some other one. There was a Nigerian Student Association over at the Student Union Building.

I only had sometime on Sundays because I used to spend countless hours steadily throughout the week and even on Saturdays writing programming codes. Writing a programming code language is more like writing a book. **It may not only need to be edited between 50 and 500 times, but also test for output accuracy.**

A month and a half later, I was doing well in all the courses but faced continuous struggling with the programming one. My vision deteriorated quickly as I used to spend 30 hours a week in the PC lab. That contributed to a **gradual body collapse** affecting the other three units' comprehension and available study time. I eventually got myself glasses.

Now, I was clearly in a **dilemma** over how to tackle such crisis. There were only 2 choices available. I had to drop the course and get a grade of discounted affecting the overall GPA. Secondly, doing nothing could cause passing the entire semester with very low marks dragging lower my last year cumulative average. Each course represents 3 credit hours. I needed to be strictly enrolled in at least 12 credit hours to be full-time; otherwise, I would become part-timer. Being along and bombarded by barriers, the essence of (C) **patience** faltered in my character.

OBSTACLES WHILE IN UNIVERSITY

Life is never an easy ride for everyone. All different milestones either in our academic or non-academic route that require significant effort can take long to finish starting from being admitted into Kindergarten till acquiring PhDs or own carpentry or trucking company, etc.., Jesus was a carpenter. "**Isn't this the carpenter? Isn't this Mary's son and the brother of James, Joseph, Judas and Simon? Aren't his sisters here with us?" And they took offense at him."** (Mark 6:3).

Nonetheless, some people believe that **being finically secure** is the answer for all our troubles. There is also a common misunderstanding that keeping your wealth within your immediate family and relatives will be your peace keeping force. Some high class ones don't even allow their sons or daughters to get married from those poor categories.

They behave as if they own the universe. However, God looks at the heart. But the Lord said to Samuel**, "Do not consider his appearance or his height, for I have rejected him. The Lord does not look at the things people look at. People look at the outward appearance, but the Lord looks at the heart."** (1 Samuel 16:7).

We have many examples of famous people who accumulated huge amounts of wealth, but they ended up losing their lives. We have examples of a Greek billionaire whose wealth grew exponentially, but his personal life was in shambles. At the end, he even actually passed away grieving on his son's horrible plane crash. Upon his death, his daughter said, "I am all alone." His widow uttered," I am the widow now."

Another example of a celebrity unquestionably regarded to be one of the greatest and most influential people of the 20th century who has earned great respect among theatre experts for his memorable performances and charismatic screen presence, he left an estate valued at $21.6 million which still earns him about 9 million yearly. He is one of the top-earning **dead** celebrities in the world.

He had a troubled daughter who eventually committed suicide after losing her lover who was shot dead being in a confrontation with his half-brother. He claimed it was all accidental because he was drunk while he was holding his gun. **I am now asking you as readers to really pray and think carefully before you decide upon what kind of career path you choose for your life.**

Whenever you start facing academic or craft difficulties, you need to be patient and give sometime to yourself to come up with a proper exist strategy from any kind of mess in which you have thrown yourself. The following steps can help you deal with some of the common university hindrances:

1. Students usually really on their own strength without seeking advices first from the Lord. Acting this why means **we don't trust Him** and he is not the primary Spiritual mentor on our list. **"In all your ways submit to him, and he will make your paths straight."** (Proverbs 3:6). This verse explains that it is crucial to depend on God with all our hearts for **His solutions**. They always coincide with **His will**. Counselling **means reading the word through which He presents His answer.** Pertaining to my third semester quandary, I became a part-time with 9 credit hours. My own **unconscious monster of depression** arose again from its deep sleep to haunt me whispering in my ears, "you are a failure", "you can't do it". It is true I didn't have any other suitable except for letting the class go, **but at least having prayed or read the word antecedently would have given me eternal peace overcoming the course distress**. It would have maintained an **appropriate balance** among my character attributes and not have left permanent **scars stored in my heart**. As always I had been a non-believer, such events greatly and periodically were disturbing my personal calmness. The scripture says, **"And the peace of God, which transcends all understanding,**

will guard your hearts and your minds in Christ Jesus." (Philippians 4:7).
2. Besides reading daily horoscopes, other ones may choose to temporarily relieve their troubles by asking a fortune teller. They even try their luck gambling in the casinos to divert their attention from the core matter. Daniel answered the king and said, **"Daniel replied, "No wise man, enchanter, magician or diviner can explain to the king the mystery he has asked about,"** (Daniel 2:27).
3. The majority of meticulous students like everything to be perfect. Some of them prefer to work alone to manage their own time. They just don't like explaining or sharing with other team members. Whereas joining a group, they can help each other in understanding and solving the task together thereby learning from each other. Additionally, the concept of unity indirectly manifests itself by getting them motivated to work, think more, and to experience constructive criticism after being very comfortable with teamwork. **Jesus washed his disciples' feet signalling the necessity of having to serve other brothers and sisters out of pure love.**
4. Being involved in some gospel's **groups renews our commitment to Christ and teaches us about our spiritual strengths and weaknesses**. It reveals the different ways of God's families function in close collaboration (with each other) to consistently develop love and respect for each other. For example, whenever a household deals with unbearable and heart-breaking events such as, the sudden passing away of a loved one or experiencing a major health dilemma, full spiritual cooperation through visiting and genuinely **sharing each other's feelings will alleviate the emotional suffering**. After all, we are all humans and prone to not fully **trusting His will in our lives because of lack of faith**. Abraham's faith became very weak when he entered Egypt after the severe drought in the land claiming his **wife, Sarah, was his sister**. He was insecure about God's protecting his family against the Pharaoh's intentions. He thought that if had presented Sarah as his wife, the

Egyptian king would have terminated Ibrahim's life for the sake of taking his wife away from him forcing her to marry him. Learning the aforementioned qualities can happen through allocating certain amount of hours per week for worship services. Eventually, this teaches us about **responsibility (strength)**. We learn how to manage our time more carefully than having to focus only on one aspect of life. Alternatively, KU has multi-national student's organizations. They have more than 15 official ones. Once we achieve some progress in one facet of any branch of our lives, the Lord will open other doors for us. The bible says, **"Whoever can be trusted with very little can also be trusted with much, and whoever is dishonest with very little will also be dishonest with much."** (Luke 16:10). Later on, we may be given a bigger task such as becoming the president of any university association.

5. Every time a track and field achieves a gold medal, there has always been a starting point in his career and an ending point. Risking permanent body injuries and fan pressure may derail her/him for a while, but she/he courageously focuses on being the first to pass. We may not win gold at the university, **we know we have to complete our mission**. A good example is Jesus Christ who **has unconditionally done His father's will. He is our highest role model**.

6. Some students like to work and study simultaneously. As long as we can achieve both efficiently and effectively, we can go ahead. Again, we have been given free will regarding our decisions. **It is essential to realize that God direct our steps for the reason that we worship Him out of love and not fear.** "In their hearts humans plan their course, but the Lord establishes their steps." (Proverbs 16:9).

7. **Jesus never gives up on us**. Despite of my continuous rejection, I even met **(6) Kasey** (not) married) and **(7) Lanny** (married with 3 children) who both strove for bringing me back to Him. We used to go on trips staying in one of his friend's homes for a couple of days. I

had the chance to meet other Christ followers with whom we would play basketball and eat Turkey together during Thanksgiving.

THE SWITCH TO CONCORDIA UNIVERSITY

As soon as I completed my third semester, I submitted an official form requesting to switch from computer science major to business administration (accounting concentration) just before the finals and Christmas break. The other two high level courses were counted towards a minor in computer science. Just as I kicked off the fourth term with a lower GPA, I felt deep inside I was a failure.

It is true we may sometimes we may mingle with other people looking at our best superficially, yet we are the only ones who know ourselves' darkest secrets, desires and defeats. Looking at pictures of naked women was the first private stuff about which I didn't want anyone to know. I began buying from time to time pornographic magazines.

Secondly, I didn't like peer pressure, it restarted kicking in. In fact, there was a fair percentage of students who were going out drinking and having fun. I had the desire of moving with a girlfriend and living together as if we had been married. In spite of our swollen conscience masterminding naughty activities, our intuition awakens our conscience right after committing a sin. Additionally, the Holy Spirit normally resides next to us but never inside our hearts as we continuously decide to live in sin.

Since I was one of them, the Holy Spirit often used to make me feel **some kind of anonymous sense of warmth each time** I became extremely angry, blasphemed and told lies, etc...In fact, that sense of judgement always talked **within my subconscious immediately after the sin** had been committed saying, "do you feel ok about yourself? "what went wrong", "Do you need help?"

I had always heard during my university early beginnings, "God loves you unconditionally", but I wasn't explained that **He doesn't like the act of sinning**. So every time sin would conquer me, the guilty feeling used to overflow my mind. Suddenly and systematically fear would overpower my mental status behaviour tormenting my soul. **So, I would love God out of being afraid of Him.** "There is no fear in love. But perfect love drives out fear, because fear has to do with punishment. The one who fears is not made perfect in love." (1 John 4:18).

Temptation always precedes sin, and it is typically a gradual process. Humans go through four steps before experiencing the ultimate aftermath of sin, which is living in outright darkness being separated from God's nature. **His character exclusively** accepts divine goodness. The scripture says, **"but each person is tempted when they are dragged away by their own evil desire and enticed. Then, after desire has conceived, it gives birth to sin; and sin, when it is full-grown, gives birth to death."** (James 1:14-16).

Having competed the fourth term, I decided to stay for one more and return to Canada. My GPA did go up, but not as much I had expected. It stabilized close to 3.23. Six months prior to my twentieth birthday, I matured into **a semi-civilized person living by the world standards.** Sin began **working on hardening my heart as my conscious wouldn't seem to bother me anymore.** To revisit, *the decisions made by my heart = An individual's Soul (thought process+ determination to do something+ emotions) + (conscience =0).*

For examples, meaningless phone conversation, clubbing, drinking, gossiping, swearing and committing fornication in my eyes were occurring sporadically (I meant looking lustfully at a women). **"But encourage one another daily, as long as it is called "Today," so that none of you may be hardened by sin's deceitfulness."** (Hebrews 3:13).

Before leaving to Canada, I had taken my fifth-semester-last-final exam around **Dec 7th, 1993**. Following this, I met a couple of my earthly friends at a café just outside KU's Student Union Building in the afternoon. Our chitchat lasted for almost 2 hours. Later on, as I was leaving my residence, I looked towards David and said, "Take Care". He replied, "Take care of yourself, Abboud."

Micheal a friend of mine whom I used to meet in the computer lab, picked me up at noon. We unloaded my entire luggage into the car. Heading towards the airport filled with nostalgia. I could recollect the first meeting with Dr. Gerald Harris, who was the director of Foreign Student Services, and ending with viewing the on-campus scenery of the vast greenish university land I had ever seen in my life.

My soul's **(D) kindness** was unexpectedly scared by some of the intense events through which I **had experienced while living in Kansas**. Although there had been a couple of good ones, but the devil very much enjoys torturing our souls reminding us that we **can never reach a sin-free** state. His job to reminds us of our **past** so that we will continuously live in our own vicious **circle of condemnation**.

The Lord says otherwise, **"Here is a trustworthy saying that deserves full acceptance: Christ Jesus came into the world to save sinners—of whom I am the worst."** (1 Timothy 1:15). Jesus didn't come to the world for the sole purpose of showing us how to live, or to challenge us to become a better people; he actually came to set us free from sin bondage so that we can have eternal life.

The plane landed in Dorval airport located in Montreal, Canada. I just made it before Christmas time. Upon uniting with my family, I still felt bewildered and left alone. More than half of my behavioural mannerisms had been replaced with eccentric ones. The devil had virtually become my master. The bible says, **"in which you used to live when you followed the ways of this world and of the ruler of the kingdom of the air, the spirit who is now at work in those who are disobedient."** (Ephesians 2:2).

Montreal is in the southwest of the province of Quebec. The city covers most of the Island of Montreal at the junction of the Saint Lawrence and Ottawa Rivers. French is the city's official language and is the language spoken at home: as Québécois French, by 56.9% of the population of the city, followed by English at 18.6% and 19.8% other languages. It is very popular for being a multicultural and metropolitan.

Canada is the 2nd largest country (after Russia). It is larger than the US by the size of Texas, and has a total population approx. 33.5 million. It is composed of 10 provinces and 3 territories. Ottawa is its National Capital. Like US states, each province/territory has its own capital as well. French and English are its official languages.

A couple of days later, while dad was having a reunion with some of his old folks, I overheard Concordia and McGill universities' names being mentioned. I learnt that Concordia was known for its commerce program branded nowadays as "John Molson School of Business" whilst McGill for its medicine, dentistry and low concentrations.

The next morning, I visited Concordia's University's admission office where the officer explained that I could enter as an independent student, but I would need to fill out *"A Transfer of Credit Sheet."* That yellow document normally lists all one's previous institution courses taken and match each one with the new institution's business department units according to the credit hours and a subject's description. Whenever there is an equivalency, a full credit is granted by the transferor.

While my KU credits were in the process of being transferred to Concordia University; I had an appointment with the student's undergraduate academic advising office placed on its first Sir George Williams Campus just in the core downtown of Montreal. It has a second campus known as Loyola College as well. It was just a Jesuit college established since 1896. It ceased to exist when it was integrated into Concordia University in 1974.

The counsellor informed me about the "Co-op Program" available for commerce majors. In a nutshell, it involves both working and studying simultaneously. The university has always offered such a program in coordination with some companies. It is usually available for those students who strongly maintain a high GPA throughout their first calendar year. Some American counter parts may provide their students a similar opportunity, but most Canadian universities including Concordia have an education structure which is different from that of the US.

As a matter of fact, Canada has a system of a 2-year college followed by a 3-year university curriculum; whereas USA has a five-year undergraduate schedule. When a student gets transferred from another university, he/she is given a new GPA. I had only 3 years remaining of study towards obtaining a Bachelor's degree in Business Administration majoring in accountancy, and I was granted a two-year college equivalency based on my prior KU courses. Concordia's minimum acceptable assignable GPA from another institution is 3.00. Because of this, I was delighted that my prior studies were taken seriously.

I still lost one semester as a result of such a process. In fact, my ego made me believe that I had received that award by my own hard work and no one else's. I should have **humbled** myself because the Lord has always shown me **His Grace since I was born**; instead, and never like ever before, material rewards had become an essential part of my life and emotional satisfaction. After all, His faithfulness towards us persists. The scripture says, **"if we are faithless, he remains faithful, for he cannot disown himself."** (2 Timothy 2:13).

The very moment we begin to take pride in our outcomes; it unquenchably leads in controlling our thoughts (**mind**), **will and feelings** = (all three composes the soul). We lose most of our spiritual progression with the Lord if any. Consequently, the devil successfully instills in us five **exemplary world-related**, and **temporal gratification** techniques in order to be increasingly enslaved by our vanity. The bible says, **"but I see another law at work in me, waging war against the law of my mind and making me a prisoner of the law of sin at work within me."** (Romans 7:23). **Egotism** is the result of viewing our **world** as our **second superior figure**.

An unhealthy self-admired character causes firstly and most importantly incorrect **human decisions**. First instance, during my first spring semester, one of my perquisites was marketing. I could recall during my first day of class the professor walking stating, "No one in this course can get an A". Despite his warning statements, I carried along with the same teacher ending up with a B-.

I should have taken him seriously the first day of class by inquiring about his teaching style. I realized that some of the classmates had had the same teacher previously. He was very moody and used to explain a 20-page marketing chapter in 10 minutes. His examples were vague and didn't fully illustrate the main points of each chapter. He would rarely have any notes written down. He didn't even know how to make students effectively participate during his class.

I had the option of dropping such course within the first week of class without affecting my overall marks or losing money, but I relied on my human strength instead. The bible says, "By myself I can do nothing; I judge only as I hear, and my judgment is just, for I seek not to please myself but him who sent me." (John 5:30).

Secondly, **arrogance awakens our fleshy desires** and stimulates our evil thoughts buried in our hearts. We become fully delighted with committing different kinds and levels of immoral acts. For example, disrespecting and lying to our parents can happen at any age. I remember once (1) stealing checks from my mother and cashing them, electronically depositing and withdrawing the funds from my account.

Shortly after that, she found about what I had done. She did ask me once, "Have you seen those checks supposed to be in the mail by the end of the month?". I replied, "No". They amounted to a couple of hundred dollars. **This situation occurred in the summer of 1994**.

On one hand, having viewed and lived next to Montreal bars, strip clubs, street drug dealers and gangs, such hangouts had never occupied any part of my mind. They were about a walking distance from our downtown residence. I used to pass weekly by them and never stopped because spending sometime in the Center Eaton Shopping Mall on the weekends was more valuable.

On the other hand, as the **forces of darkness** had smoothly **stricken me**, I was tempted each time to enter such places. For example, I once left home heading towards Jean Coutu. It is a Canadian drug store chain originally from Quebec. I came across a person who had been standing and distributing flyers for a clubbing event. It was about a club opening celebration party. Later on, I got ready and showed up over there.

Upon entering the club, I saw a huge bar area on the right hand side filled with antique chairs. The disco dancing arena was on the first floor followed by stairs leading up to the second floor. So, after I had bought myself a drink, I sat on one of the chairs. They were made from leather and very fluffy. A couple of minutes passed, looking straight through; they were a couple of guys and girls laughing loudly, and suddenly they pulled out some pills and swallowed them with their drinks.

It was hard to distinguish the colour of such tablets. Although I was very curious, I instantly remembered my mother once saying, "Dear son: never ever accept or take anything from a stranger." The **Lord faithfulness even stays towards his sinners**, and **mam's advice saved** my soul from a major disastrous situation. I was astonished to find out that consuming them can produce harmful effects. They are called **Ecstasy** today which can contain a wide mixture of substances – from **LSD, cocaine, heroin, amphetamine and methamphetamine, to rat poison**, caffeine, dog deworming substances, etc. This took place in the fall of 1994.

It is taken to increase the level of sexual stimulation. It is widely available even in the so-called decent clubs. I did end up however losing my virginity under normal circumstances. Though they were all regarded as being a **worldly-wise student experiences**, they were all pre-marital sex incidents and not accepted by the Lord. The word of God provides a testimony to the corrupt mankind's nature, **"For out of the heart come evil thoughts—murder, adultery, sexual immorality, theft, false testimony, slander."** (Matthew 15:19).

Exploring my inner-reprehensible conduct for a while, I have always heard the *famous noun phrase* "**with will and determination**" everything is possible. So, the Co-op program was available for all students who were done with their first year; indeed, I did accumulate a GPA of 3.4 which is a B+ average, I felt quite excited and personally satisfied because I was sure of being accepted over there.

However, when I presented my B+-first-year transcript to the CO-OP department head, I was immediately informed that the university only accepted a minimum GPA of A for the first year with no exceptions. I felt the biggest slap on my face towards me personally. Also, there were other students who had encountered the same situation; they were even working in non-related field and studying simultaneously; their maximum grade attainable was B+.

Not only dissatisfaction with the faculty began kicking in slowly, but also knowing that I scored some A's even while taking summer classes in my first year meant nothing to the department. Having been not accepted, another negative experience started to circulate and affect my subconscious. As a result, I lastly changed from an accounting specialization to a finance one. Also, I decided to take some acting classes for the first time in my life in Montreal Acting Studio in the summer of 1995 to fill up my sense of **utter dissolution**.

By December 21st, 1995, I had completed 2 years of studies in Concordia majoring in Finance. Obviously, my lifestyle had **become bound by sin** which is the third reaction from being a smug. Sin wasn't only amused by infiltrating my soul, it also had a venomous lethal corollary on my soul and other parts of my body. The bible says, **"but no human being can tame the tongue. It is a restless evil, full of deadly poison."** (James 3:8).

Once while I was sitting in the bus on my way to Concordia's Loyola campus, a conversation was naturally initiated between myself and my classmate. We were in the same finance class given by Dr. Sandra Button, who joined John Molson School of business in 1994 after completing her PhD at the university of British Columbia. We had to take the final exams on Dec 9th. She asked me, "What will you be doing on your Christmas Eve". I said, "I guess I will go clubbing, I heard about Thursdays". Actually it has been operating as a disco dancing club and a bar for more than 3 decades.

We had shared previously economics and finance courses together. I never missed a lecture except for being sick once. I usually used to pay attention, participate, take effective notes during lectures. She had never expected such answer from a studious individual. My answer was quite naïve and honest, but I had no idea such club was known for different kinds of one night stands about which she had previously known.

Beginning with my third year, I had turned into a person who was extremely discontent with the educational system. I was studying most of the time but not getting any kind of relevant work experience in my field. The *old popular noun phrase* had been **a big lie for the first 22** years of my life. I had the opportunity being a volunteer in the Montreal Elderly Community as an accountant for less than a week. That is about it.

However, the devil continuously presents sin as a beautiful trap. It became a kind of a **surrogate for some of my psychological issues**. I would light up a cigarette once in a blue moon to relax. I began to have a circle of friends living together without marriage. Others were solely interested in money, power and lust. I have also heard some of my professors utter extremely ridiculous and unbalanced statements.

I had once a French professor who used to be very talkative. While having a conversation about the significance of marriage, our teacher said, "The act of adultery is a temporary thing between a husband and a wife." He continued, "Either couple can enjoy themselves because it is only a quickie". It is to engage in an intercourse for a very short period of time. He added further, "They still love and respect each other". However, one of the students emotionally replied, "I thought my parents had told me that married couples are expected to uphold the law of marriage; this is called cheating." Another student added," you are physically sharing your most intimate emotions with someone else."

Hearing our teacher's point of view made me speechless that not even a single word from my mouth was spoken. We were about 20 students and only 2 openly disagreed, but the scripture says, "**Marriage should be honoured by all, and the marriage bed kept pure, for God will judge the adulterer and all the sexually immoral.**" (Hebrews 13:4).

The fourth indirect effect is living an **unstable lifestyle** which has four implied far-reaching repercussions. The human race has been suffering since the plunge of Adam and Eve from the Garden of Eden onto the earth. "**By the sweat of your brow you will eat your food until you return to the ground, since from it you were taken; for dust you are and to dust you will return.**" (Genesis 3:19).

After all, God created **us in his own image and His love**, grace and enjoyment was expressed while existing and initially walking in heaven **among His** creatures. So, any place or anything made by Him was supposed to be **peaceful, joyous and holy**. Conversely, we chose to insult the Lord's intelligence believing we know much more than him. **Our dwelling has turned into an image-based environment praising our own mini-celebrity status**. We have undoubtedly turned **His blessings** of food, health and other stuff into our human gods.

Filthiness, self-corruption, lust, unfairness, deceitfulness, ignoring orphans' rights and widows and disrespecting each other's family members encompass our advanced technological world. Our work place can be described nowadays as being the impeccable arena where bullying, mistreatment from others, power abuse, intimating statements, frequent layoffs (irrespective of someone's financial situation) are its primary leading and distinctive elements.

Alternatively, God's main goal was providing a continuous happiness for us and not a world at which pursuing happiness is an extremely stressful option. Gone are the days of having permanent careers. Everything in life has become volatile. Even those people who are journalists or broadcasters complain of too much violence and foul language on TV these days.

Technology, materialism and fame are consonantly controlling our lives nowadays. Such developments tell a separate new story of a person who discard **God's wisdom** because he suspects Him and His love causing himself to be on the run lacking a plenty of foresight. The scripture says, **"Such a person is double-minded and unstable in all they do."** (James 1:8).

The first result of having notorious fickle living is often **switching from one career to another aimlessly**. By the time more than 67% of total credits were completed, I had already begun inquiring about a future job prospects within a banks, small to medium sized corporations and government financial institutions.

During my 3rd year, upon obtaining a grade of an A in the midst of the second year with Dr. Latha Shanker, who was a research associate at the Center for the Study of Futures Markets at Columbia University and later joined Concordia University, I took trading in Financial Securities that was one of my final courses during the fall term of 1996. Besides, satisfying my degree requirements was almost accomplished pending completing it.

The finance high level lectures included attending a weekly trading session in Montreal Stock Exchange throughout the term, I was assigned to sit next to a trader who was performing real time buying and selling transactions using a variety of financial instruments such as bonds, stocks and a wide arrange of options' contracts. They are called derivatives because they are mainly derived from stocks.

Along with it, there was a homework submitted weekly. It contained an explanatory report of each trading session with the opening and closing values including some stocks' charts and their net positions after analyzing the overall gain and loss. MX is derivatives exchange headquartered in Montreal which transacts future oil, currencies, market indices, interest rates and energies as well.

Because I scored 90% with Dr. Shanker, who taught me one of the most difficult and enjoyable 400 level subjects, I decided to continue my job hunting process discussed earlier by sending resumes 4 months prior to Dec 31st, 1996. In addition, I enrolled in the Canadian Securities Course since I wanted to be a trader.

Achieving success practically and academically in 1996, I received 5 different bank interviews for a trader position. Some of the banks were Toronto Dominion Bank (TD), Montreal Stock Exchange, Royal Bank based in Toronto (RBC), London life and the National Bank. The interviews were held at a meeting hall in one of downtown Montreal hotels.

Equipped with the company's ratio analysis I had been doing along with the Canadian Securities Course, I passed MX and TD interviews, but I was not offered a third final interview or any positions in Montreal, Toronto or anywhere else. London life had a position based on selling investments and life insurance products. Besides, I already passed the first RBC phone-interview with the bank's human resources manager. Holding on to the Royal Bank success, I completed a second computerized test and passed. However, no position had really materialized. The basic trader, which is Toronto based, pays pretax earnings of $35,000 per year netting $22,000.

Basically, a monthly after tax income of $1800 isn't enough to cover rent and food in Toronto. The cost of living over there is still twice or even triple as much of that in Montreal. A room in a house in the Bathurst area could cost a student up to $500.00 per month in the basement sharing the bathrooms with 4 other individuals. Such residence is at least 1 hour away by bus and train. Alternatively, dwelling closer to downtown could cost up to $1200 a month sharing with another individual in 1996. It has more than doubled or tripled now in 2020.

There were other additional costs. For instance, the monthly bus pass would cost more than $100.00 in Toronto and less than $61.00 of than in Montreal in the 1990s. As mentioned earlier, it was known to have the cheapest rent in North America. Encountering difficulties in finding a finance job just before my graduation, I never gave up on myself, but I began listening to other people and interpreting the common idiom, "Don't put all your eggs in one basket" as jumping from one field to another.

So, I decided to meet with the undergraduate academic advisor following my parent's advice. I was informed that I could receive an additional Minor in Management Information Systems upon satisfying the requirement of an extra-4 computer science course (MIS). It would be listed under the finance field on the same certificate, but the main graduation diploma would only show a Bachelor of Commerce earned.

CANADIAN SECURITIES COURSE

This certifies that

ABBOUD R KADID

has qualified for this certificate by successfully completing The Canadian Securities Course

 **1997**

CANADIAN SECURITIES INSTITUTE

Frankly speaking, writing computer programs once again was my worst nightmare. Despite the horrible memories of spending countless hours on previous programming projects in the US, I enrolled for the January 1997 Winter session as usual in 4 Data Base MIS subjects, I was studying part-time since I had two classes per semester. A student needs to be registered for a minimum of 4 subjects to be full-time.

Meanwhile, my father once said, "getting any kind of job makes you feel better because you are accomplishing something in your life; otherwise, you mind will be full of lives' unnecessary worries and anxieties. You will end up having numerous kinds of psychological and mental problems." I did listen to his recommendation and got myself a job being a security guard manager of a high rise 19-floor-building just exactly 2 weeks passed my 24-year-old birthday. Each floor had around 12 flats.

I was responsible for a 4-level-basement parking where more than 80 cars entered and existed it daily as well. Each vehicle activities were reported and updated within a 24-hour period on my boss's office board.

I began my work on January 27th, 1997 in combination with my part-time studies. I would report to duty daily from 10:00 p.m. till 4:00 a.m.

Even though the administer of the Hotel apartments was very strict in terms of punctuality and everything else, he sometimes failed to make proper background checks on the type of tenant signing lease contracts. As long as the person looked rich from the outside, he would be eligible to move in. Indeed, we have different kinds of families from various cultures along with children residing over there.

The bible warns, **"If you show special attention to the man wearing fine clothes and say, "Here's a good seat for you," but say to the poor man, "You stand there" or "Sit on the floor by my feet," have you not discriminated among yourselves and become judges with evil thoughts?"** (James 2:3-4). Accepting a person based on her/his appearance automatically indicates that we have become our own judges. The Lord categorizes such action as being evil for it means humiliating a human being and not treating her/family equally.

Earning a biweekly check of $450.00 after tax made me feel independent, but my job's tasks weren't related to the Finance field except for monitoring and documenting the number of cars, some bookkeeping chores such accepting periodic rental checks and depositing cash in the safe. My office was located across from the Hallway office sofas' reception place. It over looked Lincoln main's street. I had an ancient-1950s typewriter as well.

The second effect **is being involved in superficial friendships and relationships**. By February 17th, 1997, I met superficial friend who used to work in a restaurant preparing fast food sandwiches. He was living alone. Whenever we met, he used to tell me in details about his experience with different kinds of women.

Once, I was invited for dinner at his place. After I had arrived over there, we had salad, some rice and chicken. Shortly after that, he showed me the Mirror's adult section. It was a very popular newspaper in Montreal. It contained the following listings:

- Body Rubs
- Strippers & Strip clubs
- Domination & Fetish
- Male & Female Escorts
- Adult Jobs

I explained to him that I was fully aware of it. Then, he grabbed his phone and called one of the escort agencies arranging for one-hour session with one of their ladies. I refused to do the same. 30 minutes later, as planned, she showed up entering his bedroom, and I just waited for him outside in his living room. Upon exiting his room, he asked, "did you know this was the fifth time? I just didn't answer him back and I left.

By March 20th, 1997, my overall (E) self-control had deteriorated. I met him again in his residence. I was part of his team for the second time around; however, I just conversed with her for an hour, paid the money and did nothing. I asked her, "why are you doing this?". She replied, "I was a nurse back home, but I got two children and my husband is a regular gambler in "Casino De Montreal."

It is open twenty-four hours a day, seven days a week whose clients are grown-ups aged 18 and older. It has been operating fully since Oct 9th, 1993. She continued, "I have to support my two little children, and I need to pay for the nursing degree over here. "I became mentally and spiritually confused about her story.

In the meantime, I was in a team of 4 students meeting all through the semester on Saturday mornings. Each one of us was assigned a specific task pertained to designing a new database system for an airline agency that used to have a huge amount of redundant information which needed to be categorized and synchronized according to different airlines reservations' systems.

Their system was sometimes very slow to respond to clients' inquiries. I was in charge of illustrating a full play of the chaos portrayed through actors (ourselves) before amendments and after. As a matter of fact, we were victorious with our project due to largely a result of our brilliant ideas, cooperation and synergy.

Not **accepting indirect advice** is the third backlash. On April 11th, 1997, returning home over with my first set of MIS final exams, I saw my sister, **(8) Judy**, rejoicing. A few moments later, she was suddenly gripped by delight again. I said to her, "I guess you have got another A." She was attending John Abbot College. It is named after John Abbot, prime minister and a former Mayor of Montreal. I congratulated her right away. She replied, "How did you know that?" I answered, "You have always been awake since 4:30 a.m. to catch up with your school work and you deserve it sister".

She said, "You too brother. You study very hard.!" I replied," not as tedious as you!" As I was heading for my room for a nap, she said, "Wait a minute". I answered, "What is the matter?" She said, "On my way back home, I came across a "Christian Gospel Church". "So, I went upstairs, and I saw a group of multiethnic people. Some of them were Chinese, Vietnamese, Canadian Italians, English and others".

Then, I interrupted by saying, "what kind of activities Do they have?" She replied, "Actually, I sat there for an hour joining their team reading and analyzing some bible verses". "I sensed some real joy in my heart especially when they said, "Hallelujah and Amen". "They have regular bible study on Fridays. "Would you like to come along?". I said, "Ok!".

On April 18th, 1997, I accompanied my sister to the Chapel. Upon arriving, we were welcomed by **(9) "David"** who was in charge of motivating the new comers. After introducing ourselves to one another, he said, "How do you feel today?" I replied, "I am good. He said, "That is great, let's pray together before studying the word of God."

As far as I could remember, we analyzed a verse in John about love. **"There is no fear in love. But perfect love drives out fear, because fear has to do with punishment. The one who fears is not made perfect in love."** (1 John 4:18). This verse reveals that only believers who truly love the Lord not **out of fear of punishment**, but out of **complete praise for his perfect love for them manifested in His Son, Jesus Christ** on the cross have sensitive and obeying hearts towards Him. It was same verse I had heard when I first attended the Christian gathering at KU 6 years ago.

Honest followers avoid any kind of acts displeasing their Lord. They usually follow constant prayer and worship out of their pure heart. **They always receive strength directly from the Holy Spirit due to receiving His grace**. Thus, their love for the Lord can cast out all terror, despair and life's distress forever. **Their hearts become a vessel through which peace, purity, joy are invariably explained**.

As a matter of choice, I was a 24-year-old individual completely separated from the Lord because I was living in error. I had no honour and admiration for Him **since I didn't love him or know how to do that**. It is impartial to say that I presented myself at the Workshop centre for some time hearing the word. I had advanced one notch up while listening and reading the scriptures.

Having a dead-end job, continuous anxiety about the current labor market had usually been the ideal stumbling blocks for a long-time. Not only such stuff but also **holding the burden of sin through various acts gradually had been building up on my spirit**. Chains of fear successfully crippled my soul and surrounded my spirit. The love of God was self-exterminated once I again I willingly left the service 2 months later. The bible says, **"Those on the rocky ground are the ones who receive the word with joy when they hear it, but they have no root. They believe for a while, but in time of testing they fall away.** "(Luke 8:13).

After expressing our temporary civilized and human happiness, each one of us left filled with more emptiness, uncertainty and mentally disoriented. According to the world, we were two consenting adults; however, the bible says, **"Food is meant for the stomach and the stomach for food"** – and God will destroy both one and the other. **The body isn't meant for sexual immorality, but for the Lord, and the Lord for the body."** (1 Corinthians 6:13).

My sister's recommendation about the Gospel's group meetings didn't **last since my thoughts were corrupt and defiled by the devil.** I even began sharing some of my experiences with other students and colleagues. Nowadays, lads love boasting about their immature and foolish experiences. Ironically working during the night shift had exposed most of their dangerous acts that I had previously denounced, but I was an **equal participant** with their destructive spiritual life.

It was around 1:40 a.m. I had finished my second round. Sitting and analyzing some paperwork I had to do, I abruptly spotted a young lady running hysterically across the hall. It was obvious she had just existed the elevator. Then, she immediately left the building. A few seconds later, another lad showed up pursuing her. She was improperly dressed. I immediately left my office and failed to get a glimpse of both of them.

I just reported the incident to my boss next morning. Surprisingly, no action was taken on his behalf. So, I took the matter personally, and I started monitoring the source of which apparently the smell of some kind of drug often circulated on the 9th floor on the weekends.

Towards in the middle of June while on duty, I received a phone call at 1:30 a.m. from a tenant who was living on the 9th floor. It was about a complaint of a very loud disco music. So, I took the lift, and I was reaching closer to my destination, a boisterous hip-hop melody could be heard. So, I knocked on apartment #912. He recognized me immediately and said, "I have a toddler who can't sleep because of such noise." I already spoke once expressing my frustration with flat #905 occupants." I am ready to call the police now."

So, I replied, "I seriously apologize", "When did this start because my last round was around 1:00 am", He said, "It all began sometime after 1:00 am." I nodded by confirming and saying," their music is all over the place." I will take care of it." So, I quickly approached such flat and knocked on the door. By the time the door was open, an excessive smoke of club-like marijuana had been there.

I strongly warned the tenant to keep it down. I warned, "the next step will be filling a report about such incident. Afterwards, I will be calling on the cops." Astonishingly, I recognized the same individual whom I saw last week running after that women smoking put inside. So, I decided to rest on the interior fire-exist alleyway stairs monitoring the situation.

Actually, I could hear nothing for the first 10 minutes, but the same pattern continued nonstop. So, I went downstairs manually. When I reached my desk, I wrote a full report. I immediately informed the former tenant to do nothing as I was about to call 911 in 3 minutes. I cautioned the latter for the last time, but he wanted to defy the rules.

The hotel had always had families and a good reputation. They never accepted singles unless in extreme cases such as, young doctors or pharmacists. Once the police arrived, everything was back to normal. However, 3 days later following this, while I was in the office duty, unexpectedly a group of more than 6 people quickly surrounded the building's entrance.

Acting calmly, I dialled emergency 911; concurrently, I didn't push on the automatic button granting no access through the entrance phone. All garage doors were properly locked. Not locking my own office door was an oversight. Surprisingly, within 3 minutes, someone who seemed to have used the elevator swiftly stormed in the office and screamed. I asked him, "Leave now". He just took the old printer and as he was trying to smash it against my desk. I grabbed it away from him, but both ends were damaged.

The moment a physical confrontation almost began to take place; the police was there. The next day afternoon, I reported to the building's manager office due to an emergency afternoon meeting. During the meeting, he insisted on having me testify in the court against what had happened as a witness. He was apparently suing for damages. He was really concerned about the $50.00 or $100-dollar loss from the apparent damage stemming from the ancient type writer machine.

His tone sounded unacceptable and harsh. I replied back angrily, "I will not expose my life for danger for some dollars; besides, those individuals may come after me anytime especially after the court proceedings." Shortly after that, I requested another meeting in his office clarifying my intentions of leaving my post. Before leaving, I needed another 4 weeks of an extra 168 hours to complete the total number of hours needed for the unemployment insurance.

During such period, I had been assigned to clean basements 1 to 4: B1-B4. I would work from 10:00 p.m. till 4:00 a.m. Sweeping dust away from a 10-year-old garage basement, collecting and emptying 20 kilos of dirt into a big black bin bags every two hours were extremely tedious tasks. It was a good workout losing between 5-7 kilos. After all, this was the first job where I had learnt how to communicate effectively with the manager.

My last day was on the 24th of July, 1997. With regards to my studies, securing the Canadian Securities Course and the Trading in Financial securities certificates in January 1997 were no longer enough requirements to compete with other finance graduates. The Charted Financial Analyst (CFA) designation became the next prestigious stipulation.

Fourthly, a shaky and risky life style exposes us to temptation. Being agnostic summarized my adult life. I wasn't at all trained spiritually to counter the world's allurement. **I had become a product of my own contaminated nature. We look so great and pretty on the outside, but we are psychologically sick from the inside.**

The Bible says, **"but your misdeeds have separated you from your God. Your sins have hidden His face from you so that you aren't heard."** (Isaiah 59:2). Being bombarded with those four fierce adversaries, the devil's goal almost matured manifesting himself throughout the supplementary different job environments.

I should have tried to comprehend the Lord's purpose in allowing me to carry up to 60 kilos per day during my first job for 30 days. He **wanted me to repent and not register for another designation.** I was trying **to make the Lord's plans and intentions match mine.** The same thing had occurred to the Jews when they lived in exile of their motherland. **"For my thoughts are not your thoughts, neither are your ways my ways," declares the LORD."** (Isaiah 55:8).

Instead of releasing my future to Him, and having faith in His timetable, I continued my vicious circle of studying and accepting any sort of gainful employment. I had a career stalemate. The bible says, **"Now faith is assurance of things hoped for, a conviction of things not seen."** (Hebrews 11:1). Since I had never believed that Christ has ever been my saver, I didn't have any kind of hope after death. **Relying on tangible material results throws away any kind of ambition in His unforeseen eternal timeline.**

For instance, not having conviction towards God and depending on my own hard work precisely resemble the same situation that had exited among Abel, Cain and the Lord. At first, Able fully believed the Lord. Then, he followed his father's steps by submitting his sacrifice which was a healthy sheep. Whereas Cain absolutely relied on sewing some vegetable seeds down. Afterwards, he collected his harvest as a form of worship.

Cain's actions are similar to mine because he felt the Lord's way of worship expressed primarily through believing and acting on His ways didn't satisfy him personally. **He overruled God's Holy methods by replacing manual chores with faith.** Likewise, I didn't consult Him, I just went back to my old habit of studying and getting odd jobs instead of trusting Him first. **"Now to the one who works, wages are not credited as a gift but as an obligation. However, to the one who does not work but trusts God who justifies the ungodly, their faith is credited as righteousness."** (Romans 4:4-5).

Committing myself to such a designation requires 20-30 weekly study hours. A CFA holder entails having key and very sensitive positions especially those ones related to portfolio management. Let's consider now a business man who owns the following shops:

- Exterior Laundry $10,000 - monthly return on investment
- Clothing stores for women and men $20,0000 - monthly ROI
- A couple of restaurants   ($5,0000) - monthly loss

Her/his goals are to maximize the source of each business income in alignment with his own long-term or short-term plan. If any one of her/his sub-business suffers from continuous and irreversible loss, then she\he'd better liquidate it to minimize the effect of the loss on the overall total return on investment. ROI equals = amount of financial gain/ total assets. So, if your net profit is $100,000, and your total assets are $300,000, your ROI would be .33 or 33 percent.

By the end of August, I had received up to 14 different books of which 10 I would be tested on. I was given one year from that date to complete level I. Levels I and II exams must be successfully passed as well. Upon completing all three levels and satisfying 3 years of a finance-related job, then earning and using the CFA title would be permitted.

My final semester was kicking off in two weeks' time side by side. I figured there was too much stuff on my plate, and I had to cool down a bit. So, I undertook to start with the designation's schedule after I had written the last-two-MIS courses on December 11th, 1997.

During my fall term, I began a relationship (F) (**adultery**) with a student thinking were going to get married sometime in the near future. We were both madly in love with each other. However, our bondage was unreal, and we had both received it only with some endeavour. Though it lasted for about 2 years, it could be labeled as, "Easy come easy go".

I had it heard so many times, "hey body: having a girlfriend will release your mutual stress, and each partner can have useful experience about life." Some others say, "Having great experience in bed is necessary before getting married". That would even confirm that abortion is justified in case the mother isn't ready. So, most of the burden is thrown at her. On the contrary, **the father is equally responsible for his actions**.

Also, research has shown that marriage rates are at their bottom percentage in the past century, still divorce is lower now than it was 30 years ago due to having fewer babies benefiting from contraceptive bills. On the other hand, **there has been a sharp rise in the number of unmarried couples living together and giving birth to babies.**

One of the parents may run away from responsibilities. That is just like the story of the 20-year-old woman whom I previously met. As a result, that will cause permanent emotional damage on the child's personality. Unless **the real father shows up, continuous and cognitive problems may persist. Large percentage of such children join gangs, or even become drug eventually homeless on the streets.** Based on an internet research done on April 20th, 2015, in the United States of America, which is by far the wealthiest country in the world, there are **about 44 million Americans** who are about to become destitute. Once they are displaced, it takes years to treat such cases.

For instance, if we don't take a shower or wash our clothes for a long time, our bodies will have a stinky and unbearable smell, a long and a good shower should be taken. Likewise, the dirty sheet needs a strong strain remover; otherwise, expect it to be thrown in the trash bin. Our sins are represented by our filthy clothes or body. They pile up to a certain point that ousting them out may take lifetime.

Fifthly, our **self-esteem becomes a function of our ego** which in turn results in permanently hating ourselves. As I gradually **headed towards losing my own self in the world, the Lord had to crush my pride totally to make me come to him**. I had experienced extreme moments of happiness and sadness over the next 12-year period. *It began from 1997 to 2009.* Likewise, 40 years of Moses's life were spent being raised as a prince. However, the other premier 40 years were spent as a humble shepherd taking care of his father-in-law's sheep.

Moses had been brought up by the Pharaoh and received the best quality of education. He had everything available in front of his disposal including being almost an heir of their royal family. On the contrary the bible says**, "By faith Moses, when he was grown up, refused to be called the son of the Pharaoh's daughter, choosing rather to be mistreated by the people of God than to enjoy the fleeting pleasures of sin."** (Hebrews 11:24-25).

That is why God indirectly crystalized **the world as one of our enemies when He was talking to Moses** about how to prove to the Israelis that he had been sent from the Lord. He revealed to Moses three acts he needed to do. For examples, when the Lord told him to throw his cane, and immediately it turned into a snake; **it symbolizes the devil as our first enemy**. Secondly, He asked to place his right-hand on his left-hand corner of his exterior chest for a couple of seconds and to remove it from which it emitted brightness. **It signified the world as our second foe**. Finally, when the water was turned into blood, **it conveys the meaning of our third spiritual villain which is sin**.

I became a 25-year-old man on January 15th, 1998. I figured that my true value was based on the kind of mobile, car, property and job I used to have. At the same time, the brand new cell phone emerged for the first time in the world markets. It was so big that it wouldn't fit into the palm of my right hand.

Materialism started to spread very quickly around the world. Other high tech gadgets were introduced to students and businesses so fast that they would become obsolete within less than 12 months' time. Employee's long-term loyalty began launching itself in all directions without any clear objectives. It usually self-terminates itself as companies were no longer interested in retaining their staff for a long-time.

Making matters worse, I thought of myself as being worthless as I couldn't achieve any dream of working and studying simultaneously. Though I was going to graduate in few months, mixed feelings of extreme happiness and sadness had been hovering over my soul. Also, my parents unceasing support including my sister's and my girlfriend's encouragement weren't able to close the **emptiness embedded between my soul and my spirit I had been truly searching for the real love within myself, but it was missing, and I gave up on finding it.**

22 July, 1998

To Whom It May Concern:

RE: Abboud Kadid

This is to certify that Concordia University awarded the following degree, to the above-named individual.

DEGREE: Bachelor of Commerce

CONCENTRATION: Major in Finance
Minor in Management Information Systems

DATE: May 29, 1998

Yours truly,

Liana Howes
Office of the Registrar

LH/mc

Admissions Office
Postal Address: P.O. Box 2900
Montreal, Quebec, Canada
H3G 2S2

ASSOCIATION FOR INVESTMENT MANAGEMENT AND RESEARCH

5 Boar's Head Lane • P.O. Box 3668 • Charlottesville, Virginia 22903-0668
Tel: 804-980-3668 • Fax: 804-980-9755 • E-Mail: info@aimr.org • Web: www.aimr.org

August 12, 1998

700050
Mr. Abboud R. Kadid
1950 Lincoln, Apartment 214
Montreal, PQ H3H 2N8
Canada

Dear Mr. Kadid:

Congratulations! I am very pleased to inform you that you passed the 1998 CFA® Level I examination. The ICFA Trustees recognize the challenge you have met and join me in congratulating you on your achievement. Your success at Level I is an important step toward becoming a CFA charterholder.

Passing Level I is a significant accomplishment. This year 59% of those candidates sitting for the Level I examination were successful in passing the exam.

Now is not too early to begin preparations for the Level II exam. Therefore, to help you plan your study, the table on the reverse side indicates those questions where your answers showed strong knowledge of the subject addressed and those questions where your answers showed weaknesses.

To enroll for 1999 Level II CFA Candidate Program, complete the enclosed Enrollment Form, and affix the adhesive label below to the designated space on page 1 of the Enrollment Form. Please note that the enrollment fee increases after October 15. The 1999 Study Outline and the book order form will be included in the Study Guide you receive upon enrolling.

Again, please accept my heartiest congratulations for a job well done.

Very truly yours,

Thomas A. Bowman, CFA
President and Chief Executive Officer

Enclosures

Affix green label below to Enrollment Form, page 1.

GRADUATION

Universities have always offered a variety of undergraduate, graduate and PhDs programs. The oldest institution is the University of Bologna, Italy. It was founded in 1088 and has about 85,500 students in its 11 schools. The second earliest is Oxford which houses the world's earliest university museum and the largest university press in the world. It also has the greatest academic library system in Britain.

I would like to express my thoughts and beliefs about why academic success in today's world can be regarded as either a **major accomplishment in certain cultures such as those in third world countries, or only as a kind of a minor achievement in North** and Latin America, **Europe, Australia** and all other nations. Let's analyses the following statistical figures:

1. There is an alarming 1 uneducated person out of 5 schooled people globally
2. In spite of a 98% illiteracy rate sweeping across three main areas of South and West Asia, Sub-Saharan Africa, and the Arab States, other developed nations are also facing some similar impediments
3. Africa, as a whole continent, has less than a 60% literacy rate
4. More than 10% of the North American population can't read

Having looked at the above numbers, acquiring a bachelor's degree can be almost an unachievable objective in certain parts of Africa due to continuous civil wars and unresolved **hate crimes spreading among their own people**. An academic holding a degree in such nations retains a competitive edge over her/his fellow high school peers. However, not all students accept such a challenge and may choose to give up after a while, especially during their first or second year. **The cost of living in those underprivileged nations is astronomical, caused by a hyper** inflationary risks and the instability of their own currency against the dollar.

Others don't feel encouraged enough to stay on at school after the age of 17, especially if they aren't really enjoying it. They believe they are better off leaving school at 16 and learning a trade: something like hairdressing, or building or carpentry. There has always been a desperate shortage of these people in the labor market.

Honestly speaking, I even once thought of ultimately becoming a home painter, an electrician or even a film director. Not being able to find a proper opening position in finance, I opted out of any full-time positions and tried my best for part-time posts.

A week just before **my 25th birthday, on January 7th, 1998**, I received a phone call for a possible job opening shortly after my last semester began in Concordia. I felt so excited because it would be beneficial towards obtaining my Charted Financial Analyst Designation, CFA Holder. It was an entry level business analyst position in a small mining firm in Montreal, Quebec.

I used to live on 1950 Lincoln Street which is the third street parallel to Sherbrook Street on which the interview was held. The latter location was 15 minutes' walk away. I arrived an hour earlier as scheduled. I was given a test containing questions about interpreting and evaluating corporations' ratios and how companies use derivatives to hedge their exposure for market uncertainty. I flourishingly answered and completed it within the allotted time.

Later on, an assistant walked out of the manager's office and said, "Congratulations Mr. Abboud, you have passed the test, just wait a few moments for the second interview". Encouraged by passing the initial screening paper test along with receiving an A with one of high level finance options course with Mrs. Shanker, I managed to pass all the interview questions except for," How many years of experience have you got?" I replied, "None". His answer," I will call you back."

Despite not leaving school at a young age, I didn't quite appreciate what I had heard. My past achievements had suddenly become a <u>stumbling block for my future</u>. I was mentally confused having no more hope in my capabilities. I didn't know anything except perusing and continuing my own way of life which had become my own creed.

Yet the scriptures say, "**When you cry out for help, let your collection of idols save you! The wind will carry all of them off, a mere breath will blow them away. But whoever takes refuge in me will inherit the land and possess my holy mountain.**" "**And it will be said: "Build up, build up, prepare the road! Remove the obstacles out of the way of my people.**" (Isaiah 57:13-14).

The truth is that the only thing that differentiates followers apart from atheists is God's being "**with them**". As the devil had been leading my life-making decisions instead of the Lord, the beast was really "with me" assuring me that my own lifestyle had been maintained equating to the real world.

By the middle of January, 1998, I was employed as a Customer Service Professional for www.sitel.com. I was responsible for making outbound calls and selling long distance plans for Sprint Canada, AT &T. My colleagues were high school drop outs. Others were simultaneously telephone agents and studying part-time at one of the universities in Montreal.

Just a couple days prior to receiving my Bachelor of Commerce Certificate from Concordia University, I quit my telemarketing job. Being present at the graduation ceremony on **May 29th, 1998,** indicated nothing significant in my life. My life seemed even more worthless.

I continued working in various kinds of jobs with no particular goal in my existence. I needed to leave my parents' home and be on my own. Indeed, I had been feeling that I was a heavy burden on them since my 20th birthday. **On June 3rd, 1998,** after passing 2 interviews, I landed a job with a very reputable insurance firm in Montreal. It is a company which offers a wide range of financial products and services that meet the needs of individuals, families and business owners.

My duties included assessing peoples' needs in terms of acquiring a suitable life insurance, investments and proper monthly payments from their lump sum retirement payments or pensions' plan accumulations.

My manager and co-workers were excellent, with a great team spirit and desire to help one another succeed.

My specific team was very vocal, and we loved to debate and give our opinions, but always in a friendly and respectful way that made the process fun. The best part of my job was the opportunity to familiarize myself with the overall Wealth Management Operations and build relationships with people at all levels of the organization.

However, one of my trainers met a 60-year-old married couple, who have always been our family friends, and managed to sell them a 20-year-life insurance policy for $150 each per month. The plan claimed a 6%-yearly-dividend payout. Once a life insurance policy is sold, the trainer receives up 50% commission, and the rest is distributed to the trainee.

Shortly after receiving a bonus, our old friend called me for an emergency meeting with his wife present. I went immediately and he said," I have heard that life insurance investments only pay out 1% annually represented by its surrender value." I was shocked and replied," I will confirm this with my manager."

Even though I did explain to my client that such value is only given in cash upon annulling the insurance contract, I wasn't positive about the precise percentage, and I didn't feel quite well about the entire sale. So the next morning, I had a talk with my manager and he said," I have never heard of such return, go back immediately, explain the misunderstanding and try not to cancel the policy if possible." Eventually, it was terminated and my old friends were fully refunded. Disillusioned, I was determined to **leave the insurance business within the next 6-month period**.

I became yet another unimportant human being in such an excruciating, unbearable world economy, but the bible says **"Indeed, the very hairs of your head are all numbered. Don't be afraid; you are worth more than many sparrows."**(Luke 12:7). The truth is that the only thing that separates devotees apart from infidels is God's **"leading them"** and **"guiding them."** because every single moment in their lives has been given a **purpose for His glory**.

I had never been aware of the fact that God is **very near to those who are really close** to Him through **fasting** and **prayer**. He evaluates us based on our intentions: he looks at the **heart**. The scripture says, "**A person may think their own ways are right, but the LORD weighs the heart.**" (Proverbs 21:2).

The fact is I had been living not only as a rationalist but also as a heart-dependent decision maker. Let's recall from Chapter 1 which defines our adolescence's **heart** is composed of: **thought** process (**mind**), willingness to do something (**will**), **emotions** and our **conscience**. My heart is a function of the first three components in addition to the conscience.

In my case, every time I make a decision regardless of the outcome, my conscience is affected which in turns influence my heart. For example, a **thought** suddenly comes to mind saying, "hey, Abboud, your body is extremely tired after a long day at work, just shut down your ears and don't listen to your loved ones." Next, I **act on** it by not listening to my wife or children once I return home.

What makes such a situation worse is that whenever my irresponsible behaviour is frequently repeated reinforcing my emotional ego, I will have gotten used to closing my ears towards other people and systematically **shutting down my conscience** of not feeling guilty at all. Mathematically speaking, my heart will produce a **negative outcome**.

This implies that our hearts is hardened, and we effectively **listen to the thoughts of the devil (our own human thoughts)**. Our spirit is made of: a. the **conscience**; b. the **transparent relationship** manifested between one's self and God via studying daily His word and lastly; c. **intuition**. Furthermore, we know that the Holy Spirit resides in the believers' hearts.

If I am not a real follower of Christ, then, the value of $a=b=0$, and my spirit=conscience; it is now inclined in the direction of my **own soul advocacy**. The Lord assists his believers by counselling and directing their **decisions and actions through the Holy Spirit** that is **linked to their hearts**. Conversely, a nonbeliever's spirit is shot down towards God; her/his life choices are inspired by her/his own selfish, lustful and earthly desires.

Analyzing my own spirit, I had never had a straight communication in the **form of advice** and influence between myself and God because the Holy Spirit **never lived** in my heart. The link **had never existed**. My heart was contaminated by my own sin and no repentance since my own moral actions had been shaped by the world's passion; in other words, I was far away from the Lord's voice, and I lived my life as **a fool relying on my heart**.

The bible says, **"He who trusts in his own heart is a fool, but he who walks wisely will be delivered."** (Proverbs 28:26). When we research carefully Kind David's life from the Old Testament, we perceive his order to count the number of fighting men in Israel was a trespass. His action was based on an impulsive resolution stemming from **his mind** (*lured by the devil*).

The bible says, **"Satan rose up against Israel and incited David to take a census of Israel."** (1 Chronicles 21:1). Despite being very bound to the Lord, his heart confided in himself (*he depended on it*). His behaviour itself would not be wrong, but the **motivation behind was greed or vanity**.

David's census was a disaster because, unlike the normal one, which the Lord has commanded in the Book of Numbers, he conducted it so that he could be proud of his military force and strength; he began to trust in his power more than on the power of God. **"So David said to Joab and the commanders of the troops, "Go and count the Israelites from Beersheba to Dan. Then report back to me so that I may know how many there are."** (1 Chronicles 21:2)

The Bible said that the devil **tempted** David to number the people of Israel. *Can the beast force people to do wrong?* Never! The evil spirit tried him by presenting only the idea, yet David is the one who decided to bow to the experience. Similarly, since the days of the Garden of Eden, the devil tempted people to sin.

However, the Lord prepared an exit strategy for David through **Joab's warning message.** Joab was not known for his adherence to the highest codes of ethics. Obviously, he had realized Israel's king motives weren't genuine and sincere. Joab replied, **"May the Lord multiply his troops a hundred times over. My lord the king, are they not all my** lord's subjects? Why does my lord want to do this? Why should he bring guilt on Israel?"(1 Chronicles 21:3). The scripture says, "For everything in the world—the lust of the flesh, the lust of the eyes, and the pride of life—comes not from the Father but from the world."(1 John 2:16). David's **arrogance** blurred his conscience failing to sway his heart into overturning his decision. **"The king's word, however, overruled Joab; so Joab left and went throughout Israel and then came back to Jerusalem."**(1 Chronicles 21:4).

Remaining confident and seemingly untroubled by **the last events**, I reverted back to proceeding with a multiple number of varied courses of actions. The first one was adjusting my resume to be up-to-date in one of the downtown Montreal employment centres. Next, I handed in my curriculum vitae to some reputable agencies.

I continued to work at the insurance company; meanwhile, **I had been preparing to sit for the CFA I exam that summer since my graduation in May**. Financial Accounting I & II, Equity and Fixed Income Asset Evaluation, Portfolio Management, Macro and Micro Economics, Ethical and Professional Standards, Global Markets and Instruments and quantitative Analysis were level I subjects.

I would read, analyze and do some exercises along with Level 1 CFA Schweser Notes Package - Kaplan Schweser - up to 6 hours daily in Concordia Library. Those notes are key components to a successful CFA® exam study program. Their basic study package combines candidates' favourite study tool, Schweser Notes™, with three full-length practice exams.

I could testify that I spent considerable amount of hours revising my entire 400-level finance undergraduate courses. Besides, estimated-400-additional hours were consumed incorporating accounting, investment and time value of money problems. As the exam date drew nearer, we had composed a team of 8 candidates. A team of two used to meet weekly rotating turns in each other's places.

During other regular weekdays, I would meet up with my girlfriend to watch a movie in one of the theatres in Montreal. On other occasions, my best friend and I would get together to watch old western movies such as, the Good, the Bad and the Ugly, A Fistful of Dollars and Dirty Harry. The Shinning, Superman movies and One Flew Over the Cuckoo's Nest were my favourites too.

My relationship with my parents entered a new phase. Despite their love and support, the sense of warmth and sincerity would sometimes be very strong, and once in a while those feelings could fade away. **Emotional emptiness and dissatisfaction** with myself had even widened further as my spiritual peacefulness continued its **vicious circle of torments**. Not only **blaming** myself for my past failures, but also accusing my own folks of that year's setbacks

My manager leaving his post just a week prior to the exam date was a severe blow to my confidence. He had done so well in the insurance business that he came to decision of running his own new office; He had built a massive loyal clientele brought about by his integrity. My faith and part of my courage had become dependent on people's character.

The bible declares, **"This is what the Lord says: "Cursed is the one who trusts in man, who draws strength from mere flesh and whose heart turns away from the Lord."** (Jeremiah 17:5).

I should have comprehended that a human is a tool in the hands of God. He is no more than a body without power due to her/his trespasses. So how an individual can depend on another human being, you may find her/him alive today and then find her/him dead tomorrow. Also, how to trust in an individual whose her/his heart may be occasionally unstable such as one's likes and dislikes keeps changing every day.

The exam was held in the University du Québec à Montréal near the **end of July, 1998,** (UQAM) in the morning; it lasted for six hours. We were a total of 15 students from Concordia, others were from HEC Montreal, and the rest came from other provinces. I knew I did well in most of the parts except for the Fixed Income asset evaluation techniques.

The Université du Québec à Montréal is a public university based in Montreal, Quebec, Canada. It is a French-language university. HEC Montréal is also another Franco business school situated in Montréal, Canada. Since its establishment in 1907, it has coached more than 78,000 students in all fields of management. HEC is the business institute division of the University of Montreal.

Amid the first week of August, anticipating my level I payoff, I came across a colleague, whom I met in Concordia during my freshman, whilst having lunch in Pizza Hot. A few moments later, he joined my table and said, "Hey, what have you been up to?" I replied," At the moment, I am in the insurance business, and I just sat for my CFA I designation exam." "Well, how about you? He vigorously answered," I just developed advanced sterilization products which can be used in corporate offices, restaurant and hotels. "I asked him," Are those cleaning products." He said, "Yes, you got it. I discovered such a unique formula that when cleaning is done, odourless smell is released. Would you like to be part of my team?" Without giving myself much thought, I answered," Sure dear, congratulations on your achievement".

Without any kind of feasibility study, we set off into the forest, I especially felt as though we were venturing into the unknown. Over again, Comfortable with my own opinion, **the lack of directing** myself towards any kinds of **divine wisdom** and the lack of **appreciation for the advice and experience of others** had been components of an irrational decision.

The Bible says, **"The fear of the Lord is the beginning of knowledge, But fools despise wisdom and instruction."** (Proverbs 1:7). A virtuous life is source of wisdom and its roots, and the evil is the source of folly. The source of my logic intuition was unstable and sometimes purely material. So, I had not in any way had any reverence for the Lord, and the consequence of my own choice was foolish.

A week later, we had an important meeting in a restaurant. Briefly after that, we headed for my friend's warehouse where he had been manufacturing and storing the cleaning products. To begin, he was importing raw materials from Brazil. Next, they would be checked for some Canadian Standard Manufacturing specifications. Following this, some other stuff was being added to the synthetic elements. The output went through a heating and cooling process. Finally, it is labeled, packaged and delivered.

Without a delay, I dived into the venture. My self-esteem was shattered and, I was insecure about myself because I couldn't be independent to live on my own. **My past mistakes formed as chains surrounding my conscience**, I couldn't move forward. So, I started <u>depending emotionally</u> on other people. I dashed around all day for the next 4 months.

Academic university level courses can be definitely useful further in our careers. I recalled taking a couple of commerce subjects during my first two years. The Four Ps of Marketing and feasibility studies were frequently discussed in the classroom. We were asked to select a specific industry. Then, we would compare the standard industry ratios with our case-assigned financial ratios for the last couple of years in order to group data together so that patterns could be diagnosed. Also, any similarities and differences in the income statement could point out some jump or collapse in sales. Accordingly, the factor/factors that caused the drop is/are analyzed, and a **revised marketing** plan through which specific **activities involved in** accomplishing particular **marketing** objectives within a set time frame are written. Let's look at the following table.

Marketing Objectives	Number of appropriate activities
Market Research	We look at the current sales in the industry, other products being sold by other competitors and their market share
Target Market	Some possible niche businesses: restaurants, hotels, universities and hospitals
Product	Disinfectant agents for restaurant dish washing machines, oven and stove, and carpet hotel cleaners
Competition	3M commercial cleaning, Ecolab International based in North America and Austin Cleaning Services located in Montreal
Promotion strategies	Achieving brand awareness via a variety of media forms, such as Advertising in TV, Montreal STM metro or in the radio.
Pricing	Cost of raw materials, taxes, insurance, labor hours worked and rent paid should be part of the price markup
Place	Product positioning aids into the development channels through which it is sold. It could be shelved in Wal-Mart
Budget	The budget needs to be realistic and balanced. Consider the measures required if there is underfunding or overfunding
Marketing Goals	A goal may be to gain at least 20 clients or sell 20 products per week
Assessing and evaluating why there is a + or − change in sales	Continuously checking with our customers ways to improve our services places us in a stronger market position

On Monday, August 10th, 1998, I picked up Montreal Yellow pages, and noted there were more than 1000 listed restaurants. I set aside 2-3 hours of day-to-day cold calling to introduce our products to the dinning business in Montreal. Simultaneously, a meeting was usually arranged within 7 days either with her/his owner or the chef. My partner's chore was to accompany me to potential client's places.

I still had my insurance office, and Mélanie was promoted to a manger replacing the previous one. I was on duty that day, but I left work right after lunch. I thought about passing home as it was on my way to my second office. I needed to get the company's sanitizer catalogue for our 3:00-o'clock-presentation appointment. Concerned about my CFA I's test result, I checked the mail box, and a letter from Association for Investment Management and Research (AIMR) read, "**Congratulations**. I am very pleased to inform you that you passed....This year 59% of those candidates sitting for the Level I examination were successful in passing."

Exceptionally cheerful, I rushed for our first-potential business deal. My partner carried on a 60-second demonstration by mopping the floor with his new chemical cleaner. Following this, I mounted the catalogue which presented the standard quantity and price for the floor cleaner. We successfully sold within the first week to **Nickels Grills & Bar**. It is a Canadian restaurant chain which has an extensive menu ranging from complete breakfasts to hamburgers, milkshakes, pizza, chicken, ribs, salads and a number of sandwiches, including Montreal-style smoked meat.

It was was originally created by Céline Dion and four other friends, who opened their first restaurant in 1990. Nickels has since expanded to 32 franchised eating places located primarily in Quebec and Ontario. Our next customer was Dundees Bar & Grill located on RueCrescent which was a 15 minute walk from home. Burgers, Seafood/ Fish, Pasta, BBQ, Sandwiches, Salads have always been his specialties.

During the first week of September, we secured 2 Nickel's chains and Champs Bar & Restaurant situated in the heart of Little Italy District in St-Laurent, Montreal. It is a 3-storey catering similar dishes like Nickels and Dundees. It is also unique because it has some deals on boxing, Hockey and soccer games from around the world broadcasting live on relatively sizeable TVs' screens.

Word of mouth was a great way to getting some referrals, but it became so slow that we were hardly breaking even. The cost of car petrol, raw materials and other fixed expenses were rising at a faster rate than that of our sales. To make matters worse, one of our Nickels managers declared bankruptcy **in November**. We were fairly small, and our sales volume percentage relied on 4 key restaurants. We needed to adopt a new strategy of gaining more customers.

We were in a dilemma about how to tackle such crisis. Neither did we have money to pay for training other sales people nor to use other costly marketing methods to attract new restaurants. We approached a couple of retailers to place our products on their shelves, but to no to avail. The fact is that a new-nameless corporation with an unknown brand name **doesn't captivate people's attention** nowadays.

Feasibility analysis should have been part of our marketing strategy. It assists in objectively and rationally uncovering the strengths and weaknesses of an existing business or proposed venture, opportunities and threats present in the environment, the resources required to carry through, and ultimately the prospects for success.

Though I was employed in three different private companies, I didn't have the required skills to be a partner. For example, when I worked as a **building administrator and a maintenance officer**, I was exposed to preliminary **time management techniques**. Learning when to **say no people** is crucial in order to be efficient and effective in handling our daily tasks on schedule.

We don't have to hurt others' feelings, but the *Lord likes his children to be extremely loyal, organized and productive in their 24-hour period*, and strongly whenever work is involved. The bible says, **"Let all things be done decently and in order."** (1 Corinthians 14:40). Similarly, faithful descendants of God are really supposed to perform their church's duties methodologically.

The **previous Client Account Representative position at Sitel** only taught me about the verbal side of communication. I learned how to select proper words to offer AT & T's existing customers new services. Achieving Sprint Canada sales' target was not enough, I needed to **stiffen the nonverbal part of the job**.

Some experts believe that body gestures roughly represent 70% of our communication. Hence, the way we express our facial expressions and when happen through our eyes, intonation of voice and avoiding being stiff. For instance, my blood vessels of my face would expand once I was angry at a situation. Alternatively, my tear glands used to be sometimes pumped on any occasion I felt sad. Mastering **stress provoking situations was left out**.

Problem solving skills go hand in hand with **negotiation**. The insurance business successfully lectured me on how to identify an indemnity need for an individual or a family, define their issue, make a list of possible solutions to it, accept an appropriate measure to deal with each unfolding situation and finally evaluating. **Creativity was sidestepped**.

Discussions can be long, but **negotiations** should be clear, brief to the point. I admit that I didn't take the insurance business seriously because of the incident that arose from greatly misrepresenting my friends' product features. As soon as conflicts occasionally arise in the workplace, the matter should be resolved on the spot; or else, it will come to be confrontational on multiple levels.

Despite restoring the first insurance case, I wasn't well prepared to lessen the number of future prospects confrontation occurrences because I **stopped looking for new clients**. Excellent negations skills are an art which demands plenty of countless hours of practice and patience. It is necessary to be open to develop other **alternatives** to the client if the proposed isn't affordable. Otherwise, **negotiations are bound to fail**, and eventually she/he will look for other businesses which can provide alternative attractive solutions, with better policy terms and lower monthly premiums.

I left the partnership a week **before Christmas Day**. In summary, the partnership failed. The scripture says, "**Jehoshaphat had riches and honour in abundance; and by marriage he allied himself with Ahab.**" (2 Chronicles 18:1). Jehoshaphat, son of Asa, was the fourth king of the Kingdom of Judah, and successor to his father. Ahab, who ruled the northern kingdom of Israel for 22 years, did more evil in the eyes of the Lord than any of those before him.

Though Jehoshaphat was very faithful to the Lord, allowing his son to marry Ahab's daughter, brought ungodly Baalism's practices to his Kingdom, and was responsible for destroying the family principles in

Judah. Also, Jehoshaphat almost lost his life when he teamed up with Ahab against Ramoth Gilead in a battle about which profit Micaiah severely warned him. He said, **"I saw all Israel scattered on the mountains, as sheep that have no shepherd. And the Lord said, 'These have no master. Let each return to his house in peace.'"**(2 Chronicles 18:16). The hostility result was that Ahab died, and God's mercy spared Jehoshaphat's life during the intensive fighting and bloodshed.

ACTING

Dreaming of some basic elementary and successful career opening position was no longer feasible as I was being bombarded by ferocious competition from experienced banking professionals. In summary, having a **plenty of education with no experience** stalled me from moving ahead. **Anxiety overtook my emotions** because my career ladder was left on hold.

I even thought to myself, "Wait minute, other solutions are available, let's gauge my employment prospects into technical posts, such as a bookkeeper, or a nurse". In a nutshell, I was a university graduate surviving outside its campus. My survival was undoubtedly questionable as external competitive **forces were pulling me towards my job uncertainty**. I was slowly drowning.

I had always been a **lost sheep that was outside His caretaker's fence**. I had never had any **protection** from foxes and thieves. I had consistently selected the wrong spiritual door to enter. Attaining Trading in Financial Securities Certificate, my finance degree with minor in management Information systems (MIS), the Canadian Securities Course and CFA I were great achievements, but didn't **awaken my heart** to really know which path of life is suitable for me.

Just as **I turned 25**, on that day, the relationship between my girlfriend and I was off. Both of us grieved, but the sentimental pain didn't last for long like the first one did since the two of us just went separate ways. Then, the sense of belonging to each other quickly eased off. Some friends were even saying, "Hey body, just move on; this is life".

Astonishingly, others advised me to get into new relationship to forget about the former one. Yet the scriptures say, **"No one sews a patch of unshrunk cloth on an old garment, for the patch will pull**

away from the garment, making the tear worse."(Matthew 9:16). Let's assume we add a tiny drop of blue ink into 2 liters of water container, the pure-whitish colour will extensively change into light blue.

For example, suppose you have had new car tires for almost 3 years. You feel that you need to change them because your tires have consumed a lot of Kilometers. Assumingly, after your dealership and other garage mechanics have confirmed your concern, you choose to change 3 out of 4 tires to save some money.

However, the Lord prohibits us from mixing the new with the old, wearing the current-style dress on top of the used one, but commands us to fully take off the gray and entirely put on the new piece of clothing. Not replacing the fourth tire could lead to a **horrible car crash.** One of my former manager's vehicle tires was blown up while driving on the highway. Next, it flipped over the highway and at the end smashed into a tree.

He survived that accident with only a very few minor injuries, but he said, "I had undergone a near-death experience". *The Lord really wants everyone to have a personal relationship with Him through reading the Gospel.* He even said, **"This is good, and pleases God our Savior, who wants all people to be saved and to come to a knowledge of the truth."** (1Timothy 2:4).

He equally **sat down and had food with transgressors.** The bible says, **"But the Pharisees and the teachers of the law muttered, "This man welcomes sinners and eats with them."**(Luke 15:2). He came to redeem people from their sins and to show them that He has always loved them since the beginning of time.

The only way **to be freed** from **the chains of sin and its death consequence** is through Him. The scripture says, **"Jesus answered, "I am the way and the truth and the life. No one comes to the Father except through me."**(John 14:6). There is one condition is that to accept His voice/ His words **into our heats by faith to clean up** our conscience (specific steps will be mentioned in Part II that goes along with the acceptance). The bible says, **"Here I am! I stand at the door and knock. If anyone hears my voice and opens the door, I will** come in and eat with that person, and they with me." (Revelation 3:20)

Despite having many opportunities to listen and apprehend the **word of God**, my pager suddenly displayed a numeric message from one of my agents. Hearing that beep again brought back my old acting memories, I decided to revive my entertainment career and again pursue it part-time to get acceptance and attention from the world.

Jesus had been waiting outside my door for so many years; still, theatre and drama carried over **immediate access** to my disoriented soul from last year. The craving for fame, which is a sin, had **once again** become the gateway to Hell or the **fallacious doorway**.

Jesus is the only Shepard **through whom** people **can have safe entrance** to His sheep. Those are His faithful followers who live **inside his barn** and under his custody. The bible says, **"Therefore Jesus said again, "Very truly I tell you, I am the gate for the sheep."**(John 10:7). The Shepard always holds **a cane** to correct his sheep's direction in case they lose it. They have to be continuously going after him. Likewise, whenever a believer drifts way from her/his appropriate Heavenly route, Jesus instantaneously brings her/him back for safekeeping with her/his brothers and sisters in Christ.

Filled with a wave of nostalgia for my old show business days, flashbacks of my early acting years with characters and events, remarkably the "good theatre and film days" got activated. Startlingly, my mental state started to improve. I recalled seeing the first acting ad in Montreal's *Mirror* newspaper in the summer of 1994.

It was a free English language substituted newsweekly founded in Montreal, Quebec, Canada which was issued every Thursday. It had a circulation of 70,000, and reached a quarter of a million readers per week. The francophone weekly Voir has ousted the Mirror on June 22, 2012.

I was 20 years old when I read the announcement. It was an 8-week course offered by an unrecognized acting studio. It was situated between my residence and a walking distance from Concordia University where I concurrently enrolled myself for the summer term. Scoring an overall B+ Grade Point Average throughout my first two semesters, I was inspired in the third-semester to attempt a managerial accounting course with which I received a mark of B in the June-July period.

The classes were being offered weekly by a 45-year-old actress who was a member of ACTRA. The Alliance of Canadian Cinema, Television and Radio Artists (ACTRA) is a Canadian labour union representing performers in English-language media. It has 22,000 members working in film, television, radio, and all other recorded media. An actor/ an actress always proceeds with The Principles of Improvisation. Improvisational theatre is the first coursework, often called improv, is a theatre class where performers act naturally without using any kind of an already-prepared-written script. Dialogue, action, story, and characters are created interdependly by the players as the events unfold instinctively and concurrently.

We were a group of 8 actors varying in ages and backgrounds. By week 8, we had had a camera class where we were directed over a 60-minute period on how to act in front of the camera. Then, our teacher commented on each one of us individually. Immediately after the class, I asked her, "How could I start my career? I have no clue."

She replied, "First of all, you need to get black and white headshots with your resume on the back, an agent and a background agent."

I said," Thank you so much."

She said, "Take care".

I turned to Montreal Yellow Pages Directory where I searched for theatre agents, then, I came across Focus International. I got the number, and called them. I had an interview the next day; the weather was cool and sunny, and it was 30 Celsius amid August. The agency was 4 blocks away from my apartment. A thirty-year-old woman look-alike, who was stylish and out of the ordinary, kind of saluted me. She said, "Have a seat please! Just wait a couple of minutes"

I sat down whilst she appeared quite busy with her delicate and valuable movie scripts being faxed in another place. A transparent glass through which I could see her was across from the reception area. As soon as the fax stopped emitting castings, she handled them by separating some of them in one pile, while others were strangely kept in a first-aid-small cupboard affixed to a wall.

Running her fingers through her long-blond hair, she suddenly rushed back to the reception area and asked, "Follow me please." The interview transpired in another agency section just next to the transmission copier. She asked," Have you got some headshots with an audition tape?"

I said, "No".

She replied, "We have a photographer who makes professional ones, but an audition video can be made by studying and analyzing thoroughly a theatre character from a play, then you can record yourself performing it solo in front of a camera. To begin with, once we get your headshots, we will be sending them to our casting directors."

I said, "Ok! I will get the first part done. I need to find other acting schools for my monologue. Thanks."

She said, "Ok! See you later!"

I tried to get some casting directors (CD) to land me roles, but they would mostly provide me with extra work. The "CD" maintains an intermediary between director, actors and their agents/managers and the studio/network to match the characters' personalities with actors' breakdown in script. The agent is the only entity that could negotiate actors' roles to "CD". When a CD is convinced by an agent's own actor, she/ he is called for an audition for that particular character. The agent's job is to make her/his client known among the utmost casting directors by pushing her/him to appear for as many auditions as possible.

I was a student at Concordia University in the fall; meanwhile, I enrolled myself in National Film Acting School on **September 10th, 1994** because the former academy closed down. It was located close to metro Côte-des-Neiges. Upon arriving to the establishment's street address, a plain-white door stood out. Just as I entered the building, I heard a loud children's voice flowing from upstairs.

For a moment, I changed my mind, but I continued going upstairs till I reached a poster of a mask which was attached on the right-hand door only. Unexpectedly, it was a bit open. Sounds of youths tapping their foot emerged from the same place. I thought I had been an intruder as I walked in straight. However, a distinctive voice came from my left-hand side said, "Hello there! How can I help you?" I turned left in no time, pacing myself 3 meters; I sat on an old-wooden chair across from her desk.

I replied," Hey! How are you?"
She answered," I am fine thanks."
I replied, "Great. My name is Abboud. What is yours?"
She answered hesitantly, "Elizabeth."
I said," I need to take some acting lessons to improve my craft."

I was really unclear about which direction to hit, but she lent me her sympathetic ear. She informed me about the entertainment business in details such as, scam agents, theatre schools and acting coaches. Her institute had a variety of professional union teachers. She recommended Bill Corday. He is an actor, known for Mr. Nobody (2009), Confessions of a Dangerous Mind (2002) and The Adventures of Pluto Nash (2002).

Scene Study Acting Level I included my first theatre role which was playing the broker in *The Madwoman of Chaillot* (French title: *La Folle de Chaillot*). It is a play, by French author Jean Giraudoux. It consists of two acts. The plot concerns an outlandish woman who lives in Paris and her clashes against the old-fashioned dominant individuals in her life. I am a meticulous stock broker whose life has always revolved around mathematical calculations.

The first part wasn't as deep and detailed as the latter one; Tennessee Williams in the Glass Menagerie was another Scene Study Acting Level I. It is a four-character recollection piece of writing by Tennessee Williams. It presents significant story parts, featuring personalities based on Williams himself, his insincere mother, and his intellectually frail sister Rose. On one hand, I was an 18-year-son who was furious at his mother because she had always desired to gain social family prestige regardless of her family situation. Conversely, I was so caring about my sister who was emotionally sick with schizophrenia.

Acting classes helped me immensely in getting rid of my shyness during my first year college. I became much more self-assured and bold in the year ending, 1994. At the same time, it was possible to say that I hadn't yet totally lost my sense of innocence. I was the type of person who would believe whatever he had heard. I could sometimes describe myself as being naïve.

When I turned 21 years old, not being accepted at the university work and study program smashed my confidence level, my sense of loyalty and trust with those undergraduate programs collapsed. Claiming the desire to take more theatre classes to restore my self-confidence back was an instantaneous "**assurance suppressant**" injection. I began gradually lowering my expectation about myself. I fed myself more negativity by surrendering my thoughts to the three-word-phrase "be more susceptible". An inner voice also said," Hey! Abboud, you don't have the initiative. Just be receptive to different kinds of life situations. **You can be a failure**! You can be a success! Who cares?", but **Jesus cares**.

The scripture says, **"For God has not given us a spirit of fear, but of power and of love and of a sound mind"** (2 Timothy 1:7). Apostle Paul clearly wrote these scriptures by the power of the Holy Spirit and under His direction. The Apostle Peter said, **"this Scripture had to be fulfilled, which the Holy Spirit spoke by the mouth of David"** (Acts 1:16). Simultaneously, he was imprisoned in Rome, and his days were numbered. The writings had been directed towards Saint Timothy who was very young and learned faith from his grandmother and his mother, which he took from early childhood. Apostle Paul was Timothy's spiritual mentor.

Although there were enormous difficulties confronting Timothy as his teacher was ready to leave the world soon without ever meeting him again, he should not be afraid and ready for serving the Lord for the following reasons:

1. God gives to his servants the **Spirit of force** if they are not averse, and trust that God gives them **Aid** to deal with life obstacles
2. He provides them with the **Spirit of love** that is capable of giving generously,
3. He **Advises** their spirit who is capable of sound judgment

My Self-respect was low because the Holy Spirit had never **dwelled in me**. God gives His Holy Spirit to His children in order to work **without**

fear of defeat in this world. Even if they go through it, they know the Lord's **greatest help has always been His Holy Spirit.** Whenever, I faced a new wave of potentially harmful circumstances, **I would not place them in front of the Lord**; I would just let them drown me all the way to the bottom. My relationship with Jesus Christ was null, and **I became steadily unhappy about myself** over the next 5-year period.

I would sometimes ask myself," How can I be a content person? I guess by helping others possibly making me satisfied. How about leaving school and getting a full-time job! Long-term's psychological sadness and suffering contribute to **hating** one's self, which in turn causes **bizarre mood swings**; eventually, this leads to personal **inferiority problems** and jealously toward others.

But Jesus is the only **Person Who delivers eternal happiness** in us. I have realized that the <u>real servants of God obviously understand that Jesus expressed His real and unconditional love for all mankind through his death on the cross</u>. They are able to accommodate their hearts with love towards Him and towards all mankind. Their **real affection and actual self-wroth is drawn from His unequivocal-unique tenderness for free by grace.** The Holy Spirit in them gives them wisdom so that decisions-made in **their lives are guided by the Holy Spirit.**

Focus International didn't have time to pay personal attention to each of one their clients since they had a range of 300 to 500 actors on their roaster. They would just provide me with extra work. I only did some background work as a hero, policeman, doctor, and a soldier in WWII in CBC Television **in 1995.** CBC TV is the Canadian Broadcasting Corporation which began operations on September 6th, 1952. Most of sets' locations were nearly inside Ritz-Carlton hotel on Sherbrook Street.

They were supposed to send me out on auditions, but I had to do it on my own. I went on for some tryouts in the beginning of 1996. Some of them were low-budget movies, and others were local theatre plays in town. Each time I used to go for a casting call, my showbiz network grew larger. In due time, I successfully changed agents **in the middle of 1996.** It was called the Zoos Talent Agency. He had only few actors; he used to submit me for various TV, Film and theatre parts available in the immediate vicinity of the city.

In the meantime, I continued my university studies full-time along with a couple of theatre advanced classes. I only registered for two Scene Study Acting level II. My third character was Clive in Cloud 9. It is a two-act play written by British playwright Caryl Churchill. Clive represents Act I's major theme: Persecution. He is the colonial oppression of the British Empire in Africa. He demands the loyalty of his family, while he himself is unfaithful to his marriage.

The fourth character was Mr. Sherman in The Owl and the Pussycat. It is a nonsense poem by Edward Lear. The Character is a striving novelist who has to work as a bookstore clerk to make just enough to get by. His *scopophilic* tattletale habitual behavior gets his neighbour kicked out from her apartment. He has a very sneaky and perverted personality. He claims his neighbour's, constant noise has made him lose his focus on his gifted writings. His neighbour is a call girl.

Zooz kept promoting my profile for different roles, but nothing happened **in 1997**. Once again, I went back to Elizabeth's National Film Acting School with Bill Corday, and got in another Scene Study Acting level III spot. I portrayed King Henry the fifth in The Lion in Winter. It is a 1966 play by James Goldman. King Henry of England has a personal clash with his wife Eleanor whom he had been detained. He has got three children. He can be described as being very spontaneous and emotional. He is a very indecisive person.

When we **put our hope in the world**, we lose because it is a beast that eats everything alive, uses it and throws it. Its values are unstable, blustery and nonsystematic. For example, The United Nations (UN) has reported that roughly 21,000 people perish every day of famine-linked reasons. A close relative of mine once said," Hey Abboud! Where is God amidst of all this misery?" I replied," Who is doing Evil: **man or God?**" *The Lord has always given me basic sense of understanding world events though I had been away from Him.*

The scripture says, **"And on the seventh day God ended His work which He had done, and He rested on the seventh day from all**

His **work which He had done."** (Genesis 2:2). After He had created everything, he rested. His comfort is embodied in a human being dominating all the animals in Heaven. They were under Adam's and Eve's command.

On the contrary, when we have turned into civilized nations, we have achieved the following:

- A new research from McGill University and the University of Minnesota published in the journal *Nature* compared the organic and traditional way of planting seed; they confirmed that unconventional farms produce 25% less harvest than that of the normal grassland.
- There are 12 highly deadly insecticides authorized for use in organic farming
- Our children are growing at faster rate and showing early signs of physical maturity
- Governments' army spending in 2012 have already been stretched to a breaking figure of $1.756 trillion = $1,756,000,000,000
- Starvation is due to by poverty and disparity, not insufficiency

Approaching the university's graduation podium **in 1998**, I shook hands with the rector, and descended quickly to the dark tunnel of the corporate world. A voice echoed," *Hey Abboud, where is your finance job? You have a telemarketing experience and you are a certified dust cleaner? You need to move out. Good luck*". I confess that my psychological wounds and pains stemming from agonizing events in my past are temporary-forgettable with time. I usually would have flashbacks of those incidents as I undergo the same problem again. When the Holy Spirit resides in our hearts, our thoughts are always peaceful in order to cope with our troubles. The scripture says, **"But the fruit of the Spirit is love, joy, peace, longsuffering, kindness, goodness, faithfulness,"** (Galatians 5:22).

After attempting my CFA I exam **in the summer of 1998**, I continued working in the insurance business. I didn't give up on my acting career though I was ready to be part of a new risky business: the cleaning industry. ASM Performing Arts was a recent training studio wholly created by professional actors 6 months ago. They were offering practical workshops on character creation, scene study, audition technique, and up to dramatic writing and basic film making.

Improvisation Level I and Scene Study II were with working actor Dean Fleming. Dean Patrick Fleming is an actor, known for The Killing Yard (2001), Assassin's Creed III (2012) and Stationery (2004). **Towards the first quarter of 1999**, I was employed as an independent insurance broker with my prior company's manager who has been operating his own ever since.

On March 17th, 1999, I left my office on Boulevard Poirier, and drove all the way to St. Patrick's Day festival. It is religious fiesta day for the leader saint of Ireland celebrating Irish culture with parades, dancing, special foods and a whole lot of green stuff. I was in Downtown Montreal celebrating with my colleagues, and suddenly my pager buzzed, but it was on a silent mode.

After 3 hours had passed, I entered into our home, but I couldn't find my mother. My pager accidentally dropped. I just noted on my pager, a voice message and a number. Her message, "Dear son, your grandfather suddenly fell off the stairs, and he was severely injured and broke his left knee; I called you to let you know. I just left to buy an airline ticket to travel as soon as possible to Aleppo, Syria because I was told he had been hospitalized in a critical condition for the past 2 days.

He was the closest person to me, and our beloved grandmother who had immensely helped while my baptism was a sweetheart. My mother once said, "Dear son, my mother loved both of you dearly. Her-without-ceasing payers for her grandchildren **have been answered by the Lord**. I always remember very well the old days when we used to chit chat together sitting on his balcony's antique wooden chairs.

I was only 4 years old when my grandfather (Anthony) would record my voice teaching me different ways of greetings. He had a journalism degree from Spain and an accounting degree from Egypt. He was trilingual in Arabic, Spanish and French. He usually said what was on his mind without favouritism. He was so generous that he would buy daily the freshest cow milk from an old farming part of town, and Arabic sweets for breakfast such as, the famous, "Fat Free Ladies Delight with cream".

My mother flew **on March 24th, 1999**. She was able to be with her father for a week till his diabetes blood sugar spired out of control causing a fatal stroke in the brain. When I received the news, I walked on Laval's Cartierville Bridge. It connects the Ahuntsic-Cartierville and the Laval(Île Jésus) district with the neighborhood of Chomedey. I had no other way of venting out except being with myself. Suddenly, I recalled the times when I would be upset with my grandfather for a silly reason.

For instance, a month before my departure to the University of Kansas, Lawrence in U.S.A., we were on vacation with the entire family in Madrid, Spain for 20 days. I just turned 18 years old. He was agitated with me; he said, "I have told you on several occasions to control your tone, and escort you mother to the bathroom whenever we are in restaurants."

It is common to generate some feelings of dissatisfaction if our parents/ grandparents correct our behaviour in the time of our adulthood. A rebellious mannerism is sometimes responsible for holding some kind of a tiny bit of grudge against them. Grown-ups who are nonbelievers are greatly prone to trimming their own level of innocence. Jesus said, **"Let the little children come to Me, and do not forbid them; for of such is the kingdom of heaven."** (Matthew 19:14).

Jesus explains that inheriting the kingdom of God requires our hearts to be exactly mimicking our children. Let's become babies again. **Their simple ways of living, happiness, loving others** and not knowing any kind of deceit, lustfulness, hate, arrogance **are characteristics exemplifying the Lord's Spiritual Kingdom**.

As months or years go by, black **spots of blame** replace their childlike hearts' (innocent) areas. Forgiving others turn into a heavy bag full of dark spaces of sin carried over their backs. However, our senses are only awakening once someone passes away because we can no longer communicate to our loved ones.

WORING IN DUBAI

When Montreal had become the place for major career setbacks, travelling to UAE emerged as a new work opportunity, I received an accounting offer from a very reputable holdings firm based in Abu-Dubai. A monthly salary of $3000.00 was promised. Not knowing the kind of living conditions over there, I left the insurance industry and everything in my hometown and flew to Abu Dhabi.

The moment I arrived, a driver picked me up. While in the car, An American-Style-Californian planted trees surrounding our way to the hotel entertained my eyes. Everything looked enjoyable at the beginning until I woke up in the middle of the night around 2:00 a.m. on some kind of a noise. I immediately got up following its source taking the escalators to the second floor. The moment I exited, a U-shaped large balcony faced me.

Then, I saw people descending downstairs from the third floor heading straight just in front of me, so I followed the crowd. We ended up in a bar full of people wearing some of the **flashiest-coloured clothes** I have ever seen in my life. Later on, some other groups walked representing various kinds of nationalities. Indeed, I was amazed by the amount of spoken accents and dialects heard.

It is absolutely true that the Hotel and the bar looked incredibly **astonishing from the outside**, but everyone seemed to have an agenda against the other individual. Happiness was mixed with **confusion expressed** in the crowd's eyes entering the bar and those staff working for the hotel.

The devil always presents a generous offer at the beginning leading eventually to spiritual death as thousands of his agents with networks work around the clock to **hinder** receiving the planned blessings from our time lines. The bible declares, **"For our struggle is not against** flesh and blood, but against the rulers, against the authorities, against the powers of this dark world and against the spiritual forces of evil in the heavenly realms." (Ephesians 6:12). On the contrary, the Lord has never stopped pouring His blessings on both the evil and good people. The scripture says, **"that you may be children of your Father in heaven. He causes his sun to rise on the evil and the good, and sends rain on the righteous and the unrighteous."** (Matthew 5:45).

Walking in the company's premises on first day of the job was very mind puzzling. I stepped in at the front door greeted very warmly by the secretary. She accompanied me all the way to the cubical junior accountant desk. Interestingly, the colleague with his thick-dark-curly eye browses just stationed in front of me said, "Good morning, how are you today". I replied, "I am fine."He said, "It is nice to see you." He immediately handed me my first chore. A few moments later, I started counting receipt numbers and boxes.

Having been present for the first 30 days, I was under the impression that the tasks I was supposed to complete everyday seemed to have been previously arranged. However, the nature of any accounting job is an art. So, your real spending number should match your budgeted one. However, I was assigned to perform a bank reconciliation.

Such activity balances the various kinds of transactions coming in and out of the bank via the company's books. All in equals all out. So, I ran across an amount for which there was a check of 60,000 dirhams withdrawn from the corporation against which only 6,000 real purchase receipts had been accounted for. A whopping 54,000 was missing. I ended up at the main bookkeeper's office where the moment he opened his drawers, I noticed many crumbling checks flying unsettled. He knew I was looking for the purchase receipts. Trying to divert my attention, I discovered that "ty" and "0" had been added to the original check of 6000. To illustrate, six+**ty** and 6000+**0**.

I moved out of the hotel after 2 months had almost passed. I was living in an apartment building having 2 bedrooms, 1 kitchen and 1 bathroom. Each one of us had his own room. Our neighbourhood was full of expats and a variety of nationalities. Interestingly, the three-tall buildings positioned on the ground formed the English letter, "L", and they were consumed by the early sunlight dusk at 4:50 a.m.

Moving on to the beginning of the 3rd month, getting to know my roommate never stopped. We would go to Dubai Mall, which is the largest one in the World and eat in the food court. He was almost double my age. So, it was fascinating to understand and observe older people's behaviour. Simultaneously, things started drastically changing at work.

Although I received a bonus for the fraud discovery, the $3000.00 monthly salary had never materialized to the promised amount. The level of accounting tasks I used to complete became almost non-existent. I became a stand-by person. Thoughts of studying the CPA (The Charted Public Accountant designation) and reinitiating my CFA Level II arose as a surface-to-air missile; however, I was exhausted spiritually and mentally.

Being one of the painkillers, jugging on Abu Dubai beach lasted for a couple of days, nothing seemed to change at work. So, I spoke with my father. We both agreed on submitting a resignation letter as my situation became idol. I Couldn't bear receiving a monthly salary of $1000.00 a month and staying with a roommate who was fully paying the rent.

Feeling handicapped in Abu-Dubai, I had no clue moving forward where my next destiny would be. The sad part I had never tried even to seek advice from God because **I had never known Him**. My spiritual relationship continued to suffer as I slowly continued sinking into the unknown world.

MOVING TO TORONTO

I came back to Montreal. I got a job in Decima Research. 6 months later, I asked to be transferred Toronto. I was in Toronto within 1 week. I only had one suit case. When the bus landed on Yonge street, shortly after that, I arrived in Hosteling International. It is a comfortable accommodation student lodge. I stayed there for 2 days.

I managed to reserve one room in a house in the Bathurst neighbourhood of Toronto. So, I took the streetcar all the way to the closet subway station. I got off at Bathurst exit. Walking for 15 minutes, I found a 2-story house. The owner was a Chinese married woman who was renting 2 other rooms at the same time. Her husband was the man who previously draw and designed the entire Toronto metro system map.

I moved into the house the same day I saw my room. Toronto gets as cold as Montreal during the beginning of the first 3 months of the year. Situated in the house basement, I slept with my winter jacket on. When I woke up in the middle of the night, I was surrounded by the newly painted four-wall-corner room, an old mattress and a small Ikea table. Feeling the cold air breeze streaming in my room, I went back to bed.

A landmark for tourists and an entertaining shopping centre, I Headed up to Honest Ed's Store on 581 Bloor St, W, Toronto, which has stuff similar to Everything-for-Dollar market. It has 3 huge floors. I bought a blanket and some basic necessary materials like razors and shaving cream. Unfortunately, we were 3 tenants living in addition to her son sharing the same bathroom. It was located on the second floor next to the third tenant who used to be a truck driver.

One day, I got off the nearest subway station to the downtown Toronto area, I landed in the Eaton's and Bay Mall. Immediately, I exited the Mall and checked out some classy suit men stores on Yonge street. Suddenly, a plenty of shirts and pants displayed outside a store's vicinity caught my eyes' attention. The store stood out as its style was very elegant and simple.

Stepping in, I was greeted by an Irish-lady with whom I spoke for 30 minutes. She suggested she would refer me to the general store manager. Few days later, I presented myself with my resume and I got the job. Unloading pants and shirts and arranging them on different racks were my primary tasks. Later on, attaching prices and building customer relationships became the most interesting assignments.

Having 2 jobs at the same time didn't satisfy my lost soul. I was still searching for something bigger than life. I started habitually reading in a library on Bathurst Area and got involved in the Toronto film festival where I met new people over there. I did some office work during the entire film festival. My life resembled a fool whose life was about to collapse. *Filling the empty broken-pieces in my heart was an illusion.*

I was trying to build back myself esteem, but my original cause of the **problems hadn't never been cured**. My entire belief system, emotions and will structure had been contaminated and derailed by my own greed. Such greed introduced and influenced by the world values first constituted my house foundations. When I was a child, my thoughts were somewhat pure. However, by the time I moved in Toronto, I turned into a 27-year-old adult whose past-unhealed sins had been totally and temporarily replaced longing for the **New World Order Success Standard.** *NWOSS.* So, the NWOSS is the overwhelming desire for more and more.

A house which has weak foundations crashes miserably. The bible says, **"But everyone who hears these words of mine and doesn't put them into practice is like a foolish man who built his house on sand."** (Matthew 7:26). One day, I woke up and began writing a script for a movie, "The Four Corners". I completed it within a 30-day period. Then, I accidentally met an ACTRA/UDA Lady from Montreal who had been living in Toronto for the past 10 years.

Such Dual Member title is given to those active performers who are part of the English and French Television Union Actor's Association.

She referred me to a Toronto-based producer who had previously completed 10 independent movies with some recognized ones on TV. I met him for 20 minutes as he seemed to have interest in the characters of the story, but he requested another rendezvous as he was going on vacation.

On the verge of an unexpected outbreak of the Severe Acute Respiratory Syndrome (SARS) due to a woman returning from Hong Kong on February 23rd, 2003, I had a phone conversation with mom who lost conscious as I refused listening to her advice to come back to Montreal. Such illness does cause major respiratory health issues causing the patient to be placed in quarantine.

As the SARS had become almost an epidemic, the world experienced a major 3-day-internet shutdown. Not concerned about my mother's feelings, I was touring intensively around my residence's back yard's house conversing for a lengthy 30 minutes with one of my old high school friends. Surprisingly, the moment we ended the discussion, mother was on the phone. She said, "I am now in Toronto, I am waiting for you, I need to see you." Overcoming my own stubborn personality,

I agreed to mom's decision to leave Toronto.

The Point of Light Part II describes details of how God begins preparing me mentally, physically (via travelling) and spiritually to hear His message to bring me to salvation in the Arabian Desert described in following 7 chapters.

CPSIA information can be obtained
at www.ICGtesting.com
Printed in the USA
BVHW030503200321
603091BV00012B/719